D0255248

Mystery
Mother

MARILYN KAYE

BANTAM BOOKS
NEW YORK • TORONTO • LONDON • SYDNEY • AUCKLAND

RL 5.5, 008–012
MYSTERY MOTHER
A Bantam Skylark Book / November 1999

ISBN 0-553-48692-6
Published simultaneously in the United States and Canada.

PRINTED IN THE UNITED STATES OF AMERICA
OPM 10 9 8 7 6 5 4 3 2 1

With hugs and kisses
to my wonderful godchildren,
Mariek and Alex Van Houten-Anselme

Mystery
Mother

one

Sitting at her bedroom desk at precisely 5:30 P.M. on Monday, Amy Candler looked at the upper left-hand corner of her personal computer screen. In less than a second, the box she'd been anticipating appeared there.

INSTANT MESSAGE FOR ACANDLER!
ERICM: HI.

Amy typed in her response, which appeared immediately in the box.

ACANDLER: HI. WHAT ARE YOU DOING?

EricM: Nothing. What are you doing?

Acandler: Nothing. How was basketball practice?

EricM: Okay. Did you get a lot of homework?

Acandler: Tons. Fifty pages to read for language arts, about a zillion math problems, and eight reflexive verbs to memorize for French.

EricM: That will take you, what, about five minutes, right?

Amy considered her response. He was exaggerating, of course. The homework would take her at least ten minutes. But she didn't like to flaunt her superior skills in front of her boyfriend. She decided to ignore his comment and moved on.

Acandler: Did you get a lot of homework?

EricM: Not too much. But I've got that paper for American history due Friday. Want to write it for me? :)

She knew he was kidding—the smiley face made out of a colon and a closing parenthesis made that clear. Amy was trying to come up with a funny reply when her concentration was interrupted.

"Amy!"

She turned to see her mother standing in her doorway, frowning.

"Are you online with Eric again?" Nancy Candler asked.

There was no point in denying it. Amy didn't bother confirming it either. Her mother had a clear, unobstructed view of the computer screen.

Nancy followed her question up with another one that didn't require an answer. "What did I tell you yesterday?"

Amy turned back to the screen and quickly typed.

ACANDLER: SORRY, GOTTA GO, PI, TTYL.

Then she signed off the server.

Ttyl was standard Internet shorthand for "talk to you later." *Pi* was their own special code. It stood for "parent interference." Eric would understand why she had to cut him off so quickly.

Nancy pushed a lock of hair away from her tired eyes. "Amy, why is it necessary for you to have an online discussion with Eric every day? He lives next door!"

Amy just shrugged. She couldn't provide an answer that Nancy would understand. How could she possibly explain that practically all Parkside Middle School students spent their evenings online with friends they'd just spent the whole day with at school?

Personally, she thought her mother was coming

down on her a little too hard. "At least I'm not talking on the phone," she said.

"Amy, it's the same thing! You're still tying up the phone line." Now Nancy's voice was getting testy. "Honestly, Amy, for someone who has an extraordinary intelligence, you can be pretty—" She caught herself in time, but Amy provided several choices for the missing word.

"Dumb? Dense? Stupid?"

Nancy sighed. "I'm sorry, honey. I've got a lot on my mind, and I'm expecting an important call."

This seemed like a perfect opening for a request Amy had been wanting to make. "You know, the Morgans got Tasha and Eric a separate phone line," she began, then stopped. It was clear from her mother's expression that Nancy knew where this was leading and was not impressed with the suggestion.

"You do *not* need a separate phone line," Nancy declared. "You just need to spend less time monopolizing the line we have." At that moment the phone rang. Nancy snatched up the extension on Amy's night table.

"Hello?" Her lips tightened. "Just a minute, Tasha." She held the phone out toward Amy. "Could you tell her you'll call her back?"

Amy took the phone. "Hi, Tasha, are you home?"

"No, I'm still at the mall with my mother. Remember those shoes we saw last weekend?"

"The platforms with the strap?"

"Yeah. Mom says I can have them, but I can't decide between the black ones and the red ones. Which do you think I should get?"

"Well, black would go with everything," Amy said, thinking fast. "But the red ones would be so amazing with your long jeans skirt."

"Amy! Please get off the phone *now!*"

"Uh-oh, I heard that," Tasha said.

"Listen, I can't talk," Amy said in a rush. "Mom needs the phone." She hung up the receiver, but now she was annoyed. It was one thing to be told to keep her conversations brief. It was another to be ordered off the phone and publicly embarrassed, even if the public consisted solely of her best friend.

She didn't have the opportunity to point this out to her mother, though, since the phone immediately rang again. Amy picked it up. "Hello?"

"Hello, Amy, this is Dr. Phyllis Crain at the university. Is your mother around?"

"Yes, Dr. Crain, she's right here."

"I'll take it in my room," Nancy said, hurrying out. Amy waited to hear the click that told her Nancy had picked up her own extension; then she hung up. What she'd *felt* like doing was slamming the phone down.

Her mood didn't improve as she started her homework. As a result it took her almost fifteen minutes to complete the assignments, and knowing that ordinary seventh-graders were probably spending more than two hours doing all that work offered little consolation. She had just finished memorizing the last reflexive French verb when her mother reappeared.

"Amy, Dr. Crain said she'd been trying to reach me for over an hour!"

"No way," Amy objected. "I wasn't online with Eric that long!" But guiltily she remembered that before Eric had connected with her, she had been checking the Web sites of all her favorite TV shows. "You know, Mom, if we had call waiting—"

"There'll be no call waiting in this house," Nancy said. "I don't want to be in the middle of an important conversation and be interrupted by one of your friends. And don't tell me again about the Morgans and their two lines. There are four people in that house and two people in this one. One line is enough for us. Now, please go set the table for dinner."

Amy glared at her mother's retreating back. Nancy had been getting on her case a lot lately. And it was getting on Amy's nerves. How could she possibly keep up with the information superhighway if she didn't go online once in a while? And why should Nancy's phone calls be considered more important than hers?

It was at tense times like this that Amy wondered

whether her emotions operated on the same superior level as her physical and intellectual skills. In any case, she needed to cool off. She got up from her desk, ran down the stairs, and hurried out the front door. She sat on the stoop and took deep breaths to calm down.

As she relaxed, her anger toward her mother began to dissolve. It wasn't as if they'd been having serious fights lately—just a lot of little disagreements. And that seemed to be a pretty common situation among girls her age. At school she was always hearing her classmates talking about confrontations with their mothers— whether over choosing clothes, using makeup, playing the stereo too loud, or watching too much TV. And, of course, tying up the phone line.

When Amy heard these stories, she always thought she was pretty lucky. Nancy was a great mother, and Amy really valued their relationship. Just a few weeks before, when Tasha and her mother had a big blowout, Amy remembered what she'd said.

"Mom and I hardly ever fight," she'd told her friend. "I think we get along better than most mothers and daughters."

"That's because she's not your birth mother," Tasha had reasoned. "Having the same blood and genes makes you fight more."

"Why?"

"I don't know. But it's true. Look at how siblings fight with each other more than with their friends. It's got to have something to do with being related."

Siblings. Being the only child in her house, Amy didn't know much about that. Or maybe she knew too much. After all, somewhere out there in the great big world, she had eleven siblings. Or maybe *siblings* wasn't the right word to use for twelve identical clones.

Still, there could be truth in what Tasha had said. Amy hadn't always gotten along with the other Amys she'd encountered. And they were the closest things to blood relations she'd ever have.

So why were she and Nancy getting into heavier warfare lately? Amy had mentioned this to Tasha earlier that day, and once again Tasha had provided an answer.

"It's puberty," Tasha had told her. "All twelve-year-old girls have wild mood swings."

Puberty was Tasha's explanation for everything that was changing in their lives. But in Amy's opinion, it was Nancy who was starting every battle. And Nancy certainly wasn't going through puberty.

The sound of a car horn made Amy look up. A bright blue convertible sports car was slowly making its way down the street. The woman behind the wheel suddenly stopped the car. She beckoned to Amy.

"Excuse me, young lady, can you help me?"

Amy rose and ambled toward the car. She admired the vehicle's sleek lines and cool headlights. As for the driver, Amy noted that the woman was very attractive, with blond hair and eyes the same color as the car.

"I'm terribly lost," the woman said. She smiled. "I think I've driven through this community about a dozen times!"

"What are you looking for?" Amy asked.

"The entrance to the freeway going north. I don't know this part of Los Angeles at all, and I've been going around in circles!"

Amy nodded understandingly. "It's pretty confusing, with all these twisting streets." She closed her eyes for a moment to get an accurate mental map of the route to the freeway. "Stay on this street for about half a mile, then take the first left after the gas station," she said. "Make a right at the second light, and when you see the big church, get into the right lane. Watch for the McDonald's. Just before you get to it, there will be an access road on the right. That takes you straight to the northbound freeway."

The woman gazed at her admiringly. "For someone who's too young to drive, you certainly give good directions."

"I've watched my mother get on the freeway a zillion times," Amy explained.

A brief shadow seemed to cross the woman's face,

but she continued to smile. "Well, your mother is very fortunate to have such an intelligent daughter. Thank you!" With a wave, she drove off.

Amy nodded, wishing her mother had been there to hear the woman's compliment. Maybe it would have reminded Nancy to appreciate her a little more.

Still, she supposed Nancy would be more impressed if she remembered to set the table for dinner. She had started back toward the house when she heard a car horn honking again. Half expecting to see the woman in the jaunty sports car, she turned. But it was only Mrs. Morgan, pulling into the driveway of the condo next to hers. Tasha was waving from the passenger seat.

"Which shoes did you get?" Amy asked as Tasha and her mother got out of the car.

"Both of them!" Tasha declared gleefully.

"They were on sale," Mrs. Morgan explained. "The second pair was half price."

"And guess what?" Tasha went on. "I'm going to get my ears pierced!"

Amy's mouth dropped open. Practically every girl they knew had pierced ears, and she and Tasha had been bugging their parents for ages to get permission. "You're kidding!"

"Well, there's a catch," Tasha said. "I have to pay for it myself."

"And you're not to have it done at the mall," Mrs. Morgan reminded her. "I want you to go to a real doctor."

"I know, I know," Tasha sighed.

"That's going to cost a lot of money," Amy said.

Tasha nodded. "About fifty dollars."

"Where are you going to get fifty dollars?"

"Not a clue," Tasha replied cheerfully. "But I'll think of something. I'm just so happy to get permission finally!"

Just then Amy's mother came out their front door, and Amy wondered if this might not be the perfect time to ask for permission herself. But one look at her mother's face convinced her otherwise.

"Amy, didn't I ask you to set the table?"

"I'm going to do it right now," Amy assured her. "Mom, Tasha's getting her ears pierced!"

"I gave in," Mrs. Morgan admitted to Nancy. "Tasha has to pay for it herself, though."

"If I come up with the money, can I get my ears pierced?" Amy asked.

"No," Nancy said. That was it—just "No," without any reason. Amy gave her mother the stoniest look she could, but her mother didn't see it. She was talking to Mrs. Morgan.

"I'd better warn you, you'll be getting a phone call from Doris Bryant today," she told Tasha's mother.

"We haven't done anything to Jeanine!" Tasha protested. "Whatever she's saying about us, it's a lie!"

"She's calling all the parents of seventh-graders at Parkside," Nancy reported.

"Can you give me a hint what it's about?" Mrs. Morgan asked.

Nancy glanced at Tasha and Amy for a moment and then relented. "Actually, she wants us to talk to our kids and ask them to be particularly kind to Jeanine. It seems that she and her husband have finally decided to tell Jeanine that she was adopted."

Mrs. Morgan gasped. "You're not serious! Jeanine is adopted and they never told her? She's twelve years old! Everyone knows you're supposed to let adopted children know about themselves as soon as possible. Most people start talking to their kids about it by the time they're two years old."

"I know," Nancy said. "I can't believe they've waited this long."

"It's going to be quite a shock for Jeanine," Mrs. Morgan commented.

Nancy nodded. "That's why her mother is calling everyone. She wants Jeanine's classmates to be sensitive to her."

Amy groaned. Having to be sensitive and nice to Jeanine Bryant would take real effort.

Nancy looked at her sharply. "Amy, Mrs. Bryant is

very concerned. This kind of information can be quite traumatic for a young person."

Amy stiffened. Her mother should know that *she* certainly didn't have to be told that this was traumatic information. Amy remembered all too well how upsetting it had been when she learned of her own birth, her own strange history.

Mrs. Morgan and Nancy had moved away from the girls and were talking quietly to each other. Tasha and Amy sat down on the Candlers' stoop.

"I can't believe it," Tasha said. "Jeanine Bryant is adopted. Not that there's anything wrong with being adopted," she added hastily. "But you know how Jeanine is. She'd be the first person at school to make fun of someone who just found out news like that."

Amy agreed. "And now we have to be supersweet to her. It's totally unfair."

"I'll bet she was totally freaked out when her parents told her," Tasha said. "I almost feel sorry for her."

"Yeah, I know what you mean," Amy admitted. "I guess we should try to forget what a nasty, awful, mean person she is."

"You want to invite her to go to the movies with us this weekend?" Tasha asked.

Amy sighed. "Yeah, okay."

"Come on, Tasha," Mrs. Morgan said. "Let's get some dinner pulled together. What do you want tonight?"

"Macaroni and cheese?" Tasha asked hopefully.

"I think that can be arranged," her mother said. "Talk to you later, Nancy. Bye, Amy."

Amy gazed at them longingly as they went into their condo. She wished she had been invited over for dinner.

"Amy, how many times do I have to ask you to set the table?"

"*Okay*, I'm going to do it *now*," Amy snapped.

"Amy! Don't speak to me in that tone of voice!" Then Nancy sighed deeply. "Sweetie, give me a break, okay? I'm under a lot of stress right now. I've got to prepare for another interview later this week."

"An interview for what?"

"The promotion to head my department! I told you about that."

"Oh. I forgot." This wasn't exactly true, since Amy remembered just about everything. She just hadn't thought it was very vital information.

Nancy spoke quietly. "Amy, this promotion is very important to me. And it should be important to you, too, because it concerns both of us. If I get this promotion, I'll be making more money, and a lot of that money will be put aside for your college education. And I'll be working harder too, so I'll need to rely on your help."

Amy knew what that meant. Housework, errands,

chores . . . personally, she'd rather give up the college education.

Nancy went back inside the house, and Amy followed her. Just as she was about to close the door, she noticed the bright blue sports car moving slowly down the street again. That woman was obviously still lost.

"Amy! The table!"

Amy clenched her fists.

"I'm *coming!*"

two 2

Amy woke up unusually hungry the next morning—probably because dinner the evening before hadn't been very appetizing. She had tried not to think about Tasha and Eric eating yummy macaroni and cheese while she had to settle for slightly burned frozen fish filets. Nancy hadn't been doing too much grocery shopping lately.

As Amy padded downstairs in slippers and bathrobe, she wondered whether she could convince her mother to make a Sunday-type breakfast. Pancakes, maybe, or French toast. So she was disappointed to see that there was almost nothing on the table in the kitchen—not even the usual glasses of juice and boxes of cereal.

There were only a container of milk and the cup of coffee Nancy was sipping from as she made marks with a pencil on a stack of papers.

At least Nancy had the courtesy to look up when Amy entered the room. "Honey, would you mind getting your own breakfast? I have to correct this résumé so that it's perfect. You wouldn't believe how picky the personnel committee at the university is. I don't want them to find one typo or misplaced comma."

"Really," Amy murmured, feeling the need to comment, even though she wasn't quite sure what her mother was talking about. She went to the cupboard and pulled out a box of cereal. Unfortunately, she pulled a little too hard and the box slipped from her hands. Half the contents spilled onto the floor.

"Amy!" Nancy wailed.

"It was an *accident*, Mom," Amy said. "I'll clean it up. Can I eat something first?" She sat down at the table and poured what was left of the cereal into her bowl. She sniffed the milk suspiciously—it really had been a while since Nancy had been to the supermarket. But it seemed to be okay, so she added it to the cereal and began to eat in silence. Nancy continued to mark her papers.

"Mom . . ."

"Hmm?"

"Did Jeanine's folks tell her about her real parents?"

Her mother's eyes remained fixed on her work and she frowned.

"Mom?"

Nancy looked up, and Amy repeated the question.

"I don't know, honey, Mrs. Bryant didn't say." Nancy groaned softly. "I don't suppose you'd be interested in memorizing all the academic rules for punctuation and then proofreading these for me?"

Amy looked at her doubtfully. "Are you serious?"

"Just kidding," her mother said quickly, but there was no humor in her eyes. She rose and gathered the papers together. "I'm going over to the university now. I'll be back around five-thirty. Please clean up the kitchen when you get home from school, okay?"

"I will," Amy said halfheartedly.

"Run the dishwasher. And don't forget to put the clean dishes away, and to sweep up the cereal."

"I *will*," Amy said again, more sharply than she'd intended.

"Honey, I really appreciate your help," Nancy said.

Amy managed a smile. "It's okay. Hey, Mom, if you get this promotion and make a lot more money, can we hire a cleaning person?"

Her mother smiled back. "We'll see," she said, and hurried out.

On the way to school, Amy and Tasha discussed Jeanine and whether they should let on that they knew about the adoption.

"I think we should wait for her to mention it first," Amy said.

Tasha agreed. "But maybe we should smile at her so she can see she's got friends."

Eric was walking with them. He couldn't understand the sudden concern Amy and Tasha had for Jeanine. "What makes you think she wants your friendship? She never did before. Anyway, I'll bet she's just as obnoxious as she's always been."

Amy shrugged. "Maybe not. Getting hit with big news like this can really change a person."

Eric didn't buy that. "So she was adopted. Lots of people are adopted. It's no big deal. This is the millennium, not the Dark Ages."

"It *can* still be a big deal, if it comes as a total shock," Tasha said. "Jeanine didn't have a clue."

"Tasha's right," Amy told Eric. "When I found out that Nancy wasn't my natural mother, I was pretty freaked out."

"That's different," Eric argued. "You didn't just find out you were adopted. You found out that you weren't even born like other people. If Jeanine had learned that she was created by a bunch of scientists fooling around with genes in a laboratory, okay, *that* would be shocking. But there's nothing weird about being adopted."

Amy raised her eyebrows. "Are you saying there *is* something weird about being a clone?"

"Yes," Eric replied promptly. "But weird in a nice way."

"Can you imagine if Jeanine discovered she had powers like you?" Tasha shuddered. "The world would not be a safe place."

Amy couldn't argue with that. "I know there's nothing strange about being adopted. But finding out that you're not the person you always thought you were can change your sense of identity."

Tasha nodded. "Which, in Jeanine's case, could be a very good thing."

Amy sighed. Actually, she agreed with Eric. She seriously doubted that Jeanine's new knowledge of herself would create a kinder, gentler Jeanine. Jeanine was by far the snootiest, nastiest, meanest, and most conceited girl in the entire seventh grade, maybe even the entire school. Maybe the whole world. She gossiped, she insulted people, and she made fun of anyone who was the least little bit different. And she'd been Amy's own personal enemy since first grade. But Amy understood what it was like to get a startling revelation about yourself. So she was willing to give Jeanine a chance.

At school, Eric went off to join his ninth-grade buddies while Tasha and Amy searched for Jeanine. They checked the rest room in the hall outside the gym first, since that was one place a person who suddenly felt sorry for herself might be hiding. Jeanine wasn't there. But she wasn't hard to find either. They found her in her usual preclass hangout—her own homeroom, which happened to be Amy's homeroom too. Jeanine was surrounded by girls who were almost as snotty and mean as she was.

It didn't take long for Tasha and Amy to realize that Jeanine was not in need of any consolation or sympathy.

"I'm so *excited*!" Jeanine was telling her friends. "I always had a funny feeling that my mother and father weren't my real parents. I mean, there's nothing wrong with them, but they're not *special*, you know? And I'm not a bit like them. My father's left-handed, and my mother's fat! When I was a little girl in beauty pageants, people were always saying they didn't know where I got my looks and my talent for singing and dancing. Guess it was obvious that it didn't come from my parents! Now it all makes sense, because they're not my birth parents, and I couldn't inherit anything from them."

"Wow," one of her buddies crooned, "can you imagine what your natural parents might be like?"

Neither Amy nor Tasha wanted to hear Jeanine's response, and they backed out of the room.

"I hate to admit it," Tasha said, "but Eric was right. She hasn't changed."

"I can't believe the way she talks about her own parents," Amy added. "Like they're strangers all of a sudden! She doesn't even *care*! All she wants to think about is how fabulous her birth parents must be."

"Did you feel different about your mother when you found out she didn't actually give birth to you?" Tasha asked.

"No," Amy said. "But it's not like I have birth parents out there somewhere."

For a brief moment, an image crossed her mind—the framed photograph of a handsome man in military uniform that used to sit in an honored position on a shelf in the kitchen. The man's name was Steven, and he was supposed to have been her father. According to the story Amy had grown up hearing, he had been killed in an automobile accident, in some foreign country, months before she was born. Now, of course, she knew the truth: The man was just someone her mother had dated a couple of times in college. It was true that he'd been killed in a car accident, but he was not Amy's father. Amy didn't have a father, any more than she had a real mother.

Later, in class, something occurred to her. It was

ironic, in a way. Her mother had been shocked that Mrs. Bryant had waited so long to tell Jeanine that she was adopted. But Nancy had waited almost as long to tell Amy the truth about herself. And she might never have done it if Amy hadn't become suspicious and started investigating her past on her own.

"A-mee!"

The accent was on the second syllable. Amy looked up to see one of her favorite teachers, elegant Madame Duquesne, looking at her with disapproval.

"A-mee, did you not hear me?" Madame Duquesne asked in her pretty French accent. "I asked for you to conjugate the verb *aller,* 'to go.' "

"*Excusez-moi, madame,*" Amy said humbly. "*Aller. Je vais, tu vas, il va, nous allons, vous allez, ils vont.*"

"*Très bien,* A-mee," Madame Duquesne said. She went on to ask another student to conjugate another verb, and Amy returned to her private thoughts.

She supposed she couldn't really blame Nancy for not telling her sooner. It couldn't have been easy for her mother to explain that Amy was the seventh of twelve clones, and that she just happened to be the one Nancy had carried out of the laboratory when it burst into flames. The fire was the result of the explosion the scientists themselves had set. When Nancy Candler and her boss, Dr. Jaleski, and all the other scientists found out that a mysterious government agency was

24

funding their project—Project Crescent—to create a master race that would take over the world, they'd destroyed the lab and sent the clones away for adoption. Nancy had kept Amy, Number Seven. But she could have just as easily have kept Number Two or Number Nine. There was no real connection between Nancy and Amy.

Except for the feelings that had grown over the years, Amy thought. When she heard the word *mother*, the image that came to mind was of Nancy. Amy resolved to be more considerate of her mother's current tension. She couldn't really understand it, though. Her mother had a perfectly good job. And while they weren't rich, Amy could usually buy a reasonable number of clothes and CDs and other necessary items. Plus, she always got a good haul at Christmas and on her birthday.

Her eyes drifted to the window and something caught her attention. The school parking lot was a short distance away, and she spotted a bright blue sports car just like the one she'd seen the afternoon before. There had to be more than one of those convertibles in Los Angeles, but she couldn't imagine any teacher at her school driving such a cool car.

three

At lunchtime, Amy passed the cafeteria table where Jeanine was regaling her friends with more fantasies about her background.

"You know Roseanne from TV? She had a baby girl before she was married, and she put her up for adoption. A newspaper found the daughter and brought them together! Wouldn't it be wild if my mother turned out to be a TV star? Not Roseanne, of course. Maybe someone like Pamela Anderson Lee. Or Gillian Anderson."

As they ate lunch, Amy reported what she'd overheard to Tasha.

"Oh, right," Tasha said sarcastically. "Jeanine Bryant

is the secret love child of Dana Scully and Fox Mulder." She rolled her eyes. "I can't believe Mrs. Bryant thought her precious daughter would be on the verge of a nervous breakdown."

"Mothers don't always know their daughters," Amy said, and realized she was thinking of her own. "Want to come over after school and help me clean the kitchen?"

"No thanks," Tasha said. "I've got a *Parkside News* meeting."

Amy was prepared to walk home alone after her last class, so she was pleasantly surprised to find Eric standing by her locker, waiting for her.

"I thought you had basketball practice," she said.

"It was canceled. Let's go home and shoot baskets."

"I have to clean the kitchen first," Amy said as they left the building together. "You know, you were right about Jeanine, she—"

"Holy cow!" Eric interrupted. "Look at *that*!"

Just in front of the school entrance, a long black stretch limousine was slowly passing. A window rolled down on the passenger side, and a boy Amy recognized as Mick Jones, one of Eric's classmates, stuck his head out.

"Hey, Morgan! Check it out! My brother's got a job as a limo driver. We're going to the mall, wanna come?"

Living in Los Angeles, near Hollywood and Beverly Hills, Amy was used to seeing limousines on the streets. But she'd never been inside one. So when Eric grabbed her hand and cried, "Let's go," she didn't resist.

The car was amazingly huge. Sitting in the backseat with Eric, Amy could see that there was room for six more people. The seats were soft and plush, the kind you could sink into, and there were two telephones, one on each side.

Buttons lined the inside, and Amy and Eric experimented to see what would happen when each one was pressed. One button opened the windows—not a big deal. But when they pressed another button, a television screen came down from the top of the car. Another button made a panel slide open, revealing a stereo system with a selection of CDs to choose from. Another button opened a cabinet and displayed a selection of bottles and glasses, and another turned out to be a mini-refrigerator. There were so many buttons, they didn't have time to test all of them before they arrived at the mall.

"You can play again on the way back," Mick told them.

Mick's brother had to be at his next job in exactly one hour, so he was going to drive them home first. "I can't be late for work," he warned them. "If you're not here in forty minutes, I'm leaving without you. Mick and I are going to check out the hardware store."

Amy and Eric promised to meet them in forty minutes and took off.

"What do you want to do?" Eric asked as they entered the main court of the mall.

"I don't care, let's just walk around," Amy replied. She rarely went to the mall on weekdays, but it was nice to amble along and window-shop without being jostled and shoved by a million shoppers toting a zillion bags.

When hunger struck, they went to the food court, and after a brief debate as to whether they wanted Chinese or Italian food, they compromised on Mexican and settled down at a table with a couple of tacos.

It was then that Amy remembered what she'd been about to tell Eric as they left school. "You were right about Jeanine. She's just as awful as she always was. Now she thinks she must have been born the child of movie stars."

"Yeah, I think I saw her parents in a *Star Wars* movie," Eric said. "What were those pointy-headed creatures called again?"

Amy laughed and they took turns naming the various characters from the movies. They started giggling, getting sillier and sillier when they imagined Jeanine as the natural child of cosmic creatures. Then Amy realized that she was being stared at.

"Ohmigod," she murmured.

"What?" Eric asked.

"That woman over there . . ." By now the woman was striding toward them with a smile.

"Why, hello there!" she said. "I *thought* you looked familiar. You're the girl who gave me directions yesterday!"

Amy nodded. "This woman was lost in our neighborhood yesterday afternoon," she explained to Eric. "She couldn't find the freeway."

"And this young lady gave me excellent directions," the woman said.

Amy was puzzled. "They couldn't have been that good. I saw you come back down our street just a little while later."

The woman hesitated and then gave a pretty, tinkling laugh. "Silly me, I'm bad at remembering directions—and at admitting it. I finally did make it home after asking two other people for help. By the way, my name is Camilla."

"I'm Amy. This is my friend Eric."

"Pleased to meet you," Camilla said to Eric, but her eyes were still on Amy. "This is quite a surprise, running into you here. With the hundreds of malls in Los Angeles, it's a real coincidence to find someone you recognize at one of them."

Amy agreed and wondered what Camilla was doing

at this particular mall. She couldn't live in this area, or she wouldn't have been lost the day before. "It's nice to see you again," she said politely.

"Yes, same here." Camilla's eyes lingered for a moment on Amy's face, and then she flashed a sweet smile. "Maybe we'll run into each other again someday. Bye!"

"I guess that's what's called a real coincidence," Amy commented as she watched the woman cross the food court.

"Yeah."

Something about Eric's tone made her look at him. He was frowning.

"What's the matter?"

"Nothing. It's just . . . well, didn't you think it was kind of weird, the way she was looking at you?"

Amy shrugged. "She was probably just startled to see me again. I'm glad I recognized her. She drives a great car."

"Oh yeah? What's special about it?"

"It's a bright blue convertible. Totally cool." After a second Amy added, "It's funny, I'd never seen one before. And today I saw another one exactly like it."

"Where?"

"In the school parking lot."

"Maybe it was the same car," Eric commented. "Did you see anyone in it?"

Amy shook her head. "No. It had to belong to some-one who works at Parkside. No one has any other rea-son to be there."

"Unless that someone is looking for you."

Amy was taken aback. "Why would she be looking for me?"

"I don't know," Eric said. "But a coincidence like that just doesn't make sense."

"Of course it doesn't make sense." Amy laughed. "That's why it's called a coincidence."

Eric didn't laugh. He leaned closer to her. "She could be one of them. You know. From the organization," he whispered.

Amy scowled. "Now you sound like my mother. I haven't been bothered by anyone from the organiza-tion in ages, not since, since—"

"Not since Wilderness Adventure," Eric reminded her. "And that wasn't so long ago."

Amy wanted to change the subject. "Eric, see those two girls over there?" she asked.

"Yeah, what about them?"

"The brown-haired one has a nice haircut."

"I guess," Eric said. "But I don't like the bangs."

"I like the rest of it, though," Amy commented. "I wonder how I would look with short hair? I've had the same long hair my whole life."

Eric didn't say anything.

"Eric? Are you listening to me? Do you think I should get my hair cut?"

Eric apparently wasn't concerned with her hair at the moment. "Amy," he said slowly, "what time is it?"

Amy looked at her watch. "Five to five. Why?"

"What time did we get here?"

Then Amy realized why he hadn't answered her question. With a gasp, she leaped up from her seat. Together they ran from the food court, through a store, across the mall's main court, and out into the parking lot.

"Oh no," Eric groaned, and he didn't have to say why he was upset. Amy too could see that the black stretch limo was gone. She echoed his groan.

"My mother's going to kill me if I'm not there when she gets home. Can you call your mother to come pick us up?"

"She's not home," Eric said glumly. He reached into his pocket and pulled out a handful of change. "You got any money for a cab?"

Amy looked. "Not enough."

Which meant that they had to rely on public transportation. And in Los Angeles that meant buses. They waited for one bus, and then waited some more to catch another. By the time they got off at the stop closest to their homes, forty-five minutes had passed.

"It's only quarter of six," Eric said. "Not even dinner-time. We're fine."

"*You're* fine," Amy replied grimly. "I'm not so sure about me."

And she was right. Nancy Candler wasn't just annoyed—she was mad.

"Amy, you told me you were coming straight home from school! Where were you?"

Amy went on the defensive. "I went to the mall with Eric. I hardly have any homework, and we got a ride in a limousine. The brother of a friend of Eric's drives it for his job. What's the big deal?"

Her mother pointed wordlessly to the kitchen. Amy remembered the cereal and the dirty dishes.

"Oops! Sorry, I forgot."

"You forgot to make your bed, too," her mother pointed out.

"It's *my* bed," Amy said. "I shouldn't have to make it if I don't want to."

"Well, *I* want you to make it," Nancy declared. "We have rules in this house, and you know perfectly well what they are!"

"Okay, okay," Amy snapped. "I said I was sorry!" She stormed upstairs to her room and flung herself on the unmade bed.

It wasn't fair, it just wasn't fair. She knew she should

have remembered about cleaning the kitchen and making her bed. But she knew the real reason her mother was upset. It was because Amy hadn't called to let her know where she was. That was the part that wasn't fair. Other kids didn't have to inform their parents about every move they made.

But other kids weren't clones. Other kids weren't in constant danger.

The organization hadn't sent anyone to abduct her in a long while, but she knew they were out there. Watching. Waiting. Wanting her—or someone just like her.

Back when her mother, Dr. Jaleski, and the other scientists had destroyed Project Crescent by blowing up the laboratory, they'd hoped the organization would think all the clones had died in the explosion. For twelve years Nancy Candler had been convinced that they'd succeeded in their deception.

But she had found out she was wrong. They knew—or at least they suspected—that the clones had survived. That they were out there somewhere—the twelve Amy clones with identical crescent moons on their right shoulder blades. Girls with superior abilities and memories and intelligence. Maybe some boys, too. And the organization hadn't given up its goal to create a master race to take over the world.

That was why her mother worried about where Amy was at all times. That was why Nancy wouldn't let her get a haircut. Or a manicure, either. DNA could be identified through hair samples and fingernail clippings. Nancy didn't want anyone to have the chance to confirm what Amy was.

Amy tried not to think about it all too much. It was a secret she needed to keep for her safety—for her very survival, although she had confided in Tasha and Eric. They knew the truth about her, but she trusted them, and she was grateful that most of the time they forgot she was a clone.

She just wished her mother would forget too.

four

Eric had early-morning basketball practice the next day to make up for the cancellation the afternoon before, so Amy and Tasha walked to school without him. This was good, since Tasha only wanted to talk about pierced ears. She debated the pros and cons of tiny silver loops versus little gold balls.

Amy listened to her halfheartedly. She couldn't help feeling a twinge of jealousy.

Tasha tried to be optimistic. "Your mother could change her mind," she said. "When she gets this new job, she'll be in a better mood."

"*If* she gets the job," Amy corrected her. "If she doesn't, she'll be in a worse mood than she's in now.

And if she does get the job, she'll probably be working so hard, she'll still be in a bad mood."

"Think positively," Tasha advised. "Maybe when she sees me with my pierced ears, she'll realize it's not a big deal."

"For you maybe," Amy replied glumly. "But it's not going to change anything for me. She'll *never* let me get my ears pierced. She doesn't like me to get anywhere near doctors. She's always afraid that they'll figure out what I am and stick me in a hospital for tests and experiments."

"You don't have to go to a doctor," Tasha pointed out. "There's the place at the mall that will do it for free if you buy a pair of earrings. I wish my mom would let me do that, so I wouldn't have to pay a fortune to go to a doctor. But she's worried I'll get an infection."

Amy sighed. "My mother doesn't even have to worry about that. I've got such a superior immune system that I can't get an infection. I think she just doesn't want me to grow up. As if pierced ears make you look ten years older or something. You're lucky to have a normal mother, Tasha." After a moment she added, "You're lucky to *be* normal."

"Right," Tasha declared dryly. "So I can spend an hour memorizing South American exports while you do it in five minutes."

"But at least you'll be able to memorize with your ears pierced."

"Right," Tasha said again. "But I still have to figure out how I'm going to get the money. And not just for the doctor. Now my mother says I have to wear real gold or silver earrings. Not just gold plate, either. And those are going to cost another fifty dollars."

"Don't you have any allowance saved up?"

"I blew it all on those shoes. I even had to get an advance on the next two weeks' allowances. I only make four dollars an hour baby-sitting, and I don't get that many jobs anyway. It could take me *months* to save up."

Amy wished she could come up with a helpful suggestion, but she couldn't think of any. There weren't very many ways for kids their age to make money. "I'd lend you my allowance," she said, "but I'm saving for something too."

"What?"

"A haircut."

Tasha was surprised. "Your mother won't let you get your ears pierced, but she said you could get a haircut?"

"Well, not exactly. But if I go ahead and cut my hair, there won't be anything she can do about it."

"Amy! Are you crazy? Your mother will go nuts!"

"She's half nuts already, so what's the difference?" Amy grumbled. But Tasha was right. Would Amy really have the guts to defy her mother like that?

As they rounded the corner to the main entrance of Parkside, they were both startled to see Jeanine sitting on the front steps. This was the area where the very popular crowd from the ninth grade hung out, and only a few younger students were permitted to join them. Amy recognized Tracee Bell, a ninth-grader who had failed French twice and who was in Amy's seventh-grade French class. Tracee wasn't too intelligent, but she was friendlier than the others in that crowd.

Jeanine had tried hanging out with them once before, but she'd gotten on the nerves of one of the leading members and had been sent away. But that particular member of the crowd was now at another school, so apparently Jeanine was making another attempt to fit in. She was using her new prestige as a mysterious love child as the key.

From where she and Tasha stood, Amy could hear Jeanine speaking in a solemn tone. "I'm going to search the whole planet Earth over for my true parents. I don't care how long it takes. Someday I'll find them."

Amy reported what only she could hear to Tasha, who laughed. "She'd better expand her search beyond Earth. I know those parents have to be living on some other planet. What else is she saying?"

Amy concentrated. "She's telling them she might be royalty—like a French princess."

Tasha snorted. "What a dummy. There are no

princesses in France. They had a revolution to get rid of all their royalty."

Amy recalled reading a novel about this. "That's when Marie Antoinette was sent to the guillotine and her head was cut off."

"Exactly," Tasha said. Her eyes lit up. "Hey, Jeanine could be a direct descendant of Marie Antoinette. Maybe if she goes to France, they'll cut her head off too." They were now almost at the foot of the steps, and she too could hear Jeanine's fantasies.

"I'm sure there must have been a good reason for them to give me up," Jeanine was saying. "Like, maybe I would have caused some international scandal."

"Exactly how are you going to find your parents?" Tracee asked with mild interest.

"I'm going to hire a private detective."

"That's expensive," Tracee said.

"I have a very good allowance," Jeanine told her. "My parents—well, I guess I should say the people who adopted me—are very generous."

"They'd better be generous," someone else said. "My mother hired a detective once, when she was getting a divorce from my father. It cost her a hundred dollars a day."

Jeanine actually went a little pale. "A hundred dollars a day?" she repeated.

Tracee spotted Amy and Tasha coming up the steps.

"Hi, Amy!" she called. "Could you meet me before class and listen to me recite my congregations?"

"*Conjugations,*" Amy corrected her. "Sure, Tracee." She thought Tracee's English was almost as bad as her French. But the poor girl was seriously trying to pass the course so she could go on to high school next September with her friends.

Jeanine looked mildly impressed to see that one of the popular crowd was so friendly with Amy. Amy didn't care—but Tasha stepped forward and spoke to Jeanine unexpectedly.

"You know, Jeanine, you don't really need a private detective to find your natural parents. All you need is someone who knows how to research leads."

Jeanine stared at her uncomprehendingly. But one of the ninth-graders spoke up in support. "That's true. I saw something on *The Ricki Lake Show* about how these twins were separated at birth but found each other on their own through the Internet."

"That wasn't on Ricki Lake," Tracee said. "It was on Jenny Jones."

It didn't really matter to Jeanine which talk show the report had appeared on. She was actually looking interested. She addressed the popular crowd. "I don't have time to fool around on the Internet. But I could pay a computer nerd to do it for me."

"*I could do it for you,*" Tasha offered. A giggle went through the group, as Tasha had just clearly identified herself as a nerd. But Tasha didn't seem to care, and Amy knew why. Here was a chance to make some money.

Jeanine gazed at her suspiciously. "You know how to do stuff like that?"

"Of course Tasha knows," Amy said. "No kidding! Tasha is a whiz at surfing the Net. That's what detectives do."

Jeanine examined Tasha through narrowed eyes. "I'm not paying you a hundred dollars a day."

"What can you pay me?" Tasha asked her.

Jeanine considered this. "Five dollars a day."

"Ten," Tasha countered.

Jeanine snorted. "Forget it."

"With a guarantee," Tasha added. "If I don't find at least one of your parents, you'll get half your money back."

"That sounds like a pretty good deal to me," a ninth-grade boy piped up.

Amy was pleased because she knew there was no way that Jeanine would disregard the opinion of a very good-looking athletic ninth-grader of the opposite sex.

Sure enough, Jeanine was nodding, if a little reluctantly. "Okay." She reached into her bag and took out ten dollars. "And you start today. But if you don't find one of my parents in a week, that's it."

"Deal," Tasha said, happily taking the money.

Personally, Amy thought Tasha was being rash in agreeing to Jeanine's conditions. Still, Tasha was certainly getting a lot closer to having her ears pierced.

f i v e

"Do you really think you'll find Jeanine's parents in a week?" Amy asked as she and Tasha walked home from school that afternoon.

"Hard to say, but anything's possible." Tasha smiled. "At least it'll be fun checking out all these Web sites I've never seen before. Besides, I'll make at least thirty-five dollars."

Amy couldn't argue that. Things were looking up for Tasha either way.

When they came around the corner near their condos, Amy saw her mother's car in the driveway. The last thing she wanted was to go home and listen to her mother nag. "Want to do something at your place?" she asked Tasha.

"Sorry, Amy, I want to get started searching."

Amy sighed. Eric had his usual basketball practice, so there was no one for her to hang out with. "Can I come over and watch you?"

"Sure," Tasha said.

Amy called her mother to say she was at Tasha's, but it wasn't very interesting to watch her best friend stare at a computer screen. Restlessly Amy wandered around Tasha's room, which she knew just about as well as her own. Then she moved out into the hallway.

She noticed a large box containing jars and bottles. "What's this stuff, Tasha?" she called out.

Tasha glanced away from the computer to see what Amy was talking about. "Oh, it's stuff from the cabinets in the bathroom. Mom was cleaning it out yesterday."

Amy picked up one of the bottles. It was half full of some sort of rose-scented bath oil. She unscrewed the top and took a whiff. It was disgusting.

She poked around the other stuff. There were some old cosmetics, a jar of brown gook that claimed to remove wrinkles, and bottles that contained hardened bits of nail polish.

But there was one small box that appeared to be intact and unopened. Amy picked it up and brought it over to Tasha. "Whose is this? It looks new."

Tasha tore herself away from the screen and examined the box in Amy's hand. Her brow furrowed in puzzlement and then smoothed. "Oh! I remember." The memory made her giggle. "My mother found these gray hairs, and she wanted to get rid of them. She decided that if she was going to put color on her hair, she might as well go a little wild. It's red hair dye."

"But she didn't use it?"

"Nah. Dad took one look at the picture on the box and said he'd divorce her if she dyed her hair that color. I was younger, and I remember being worried, because I didn't know he was kidding."

Amy examined the picture of the red-haired woman on the box. "It's not so bad. I kind of like it." But by now Tasha's focus was once again on the computer screen, and she didn't respond.

Amy sat down on one of the twin beds and looked at the picture for a while. Then she opened the box. Inside she found two plastic bottles, one larger than the other, and a pair of plastic gloves. There was also a sheet of instructions.

Amy read the sheet. It looked remarkably easy to her. All she had to do was put on the plastic gloves, cut off the plastic tip of the larger bottle, pour the stuff from the smaller bottle into the larger bottle, and shake it up. Then the instructions said to squeeze the mixture onto your hair and leave it there for twenty minutes. After that, you rinsed it out. And presto! You were a dazzling redhead.

Amy got up and went to the mirror that hung over Tasha's dresser. Her brown hair hung straight to well below her shoulders. Every other month her mother trimmed it straight across to keep it that length. No one else was allowed to cut Amy's hair.

She was forbidden to change her hairstyle. But Nancy had never said anything about the color.

A smile crept onto Amy's face. There was no one else home at the Morgans', and the bathroom was free for at least half an hour. And she was bored.

Without bothering to disturb Tasha again, Amy took the hair dye into the bathroom. She clipped the top of the larger bottle, poured in the contents of the smaller bottle, and even remembered to put a gloved finger over the tip of the large bottle while she shook it up. Then she began applying the brownish gunk to her hair.

It was a thick liquid, almost like mud, and it didn't drip at all. It didn't look very powerful either—in fact, the stuff was just about the same color as her own hair. It dawned on her that the dye was pretty old and might have lost its effectiveness. But she followed the instructions, covering her hair with the gooey dye and then piling it on top of her head.

The Morgans kept magazines in a basket by the toilet, so Amy selected one and sat down on the edge of the tub to read and wait. Twenty minutes, the instructions said.

With her advanced intellect, Amy could read extremely fast. And she used this skill when she had to read boring stuff like textbooks. But she preferred to read like an ordinary person when she was reading for pleasure. The article she selected was interesting—it was all about teenage runaways who lived on the streets of Los Angeles. So Amy put her brain in "normal" mode and read at an ordinary pace.

The life of the runaways sounded pretty grim. They slept in alleys and under bridges. They were scared and dirty and they never had enough to eat. Half of them were doing drugs. The descriptions of their awful existence kept her glued to the pages. No matter how bad things got at home, Amy couldn't imagine running away and living hand to mouth.

When she remembered to check her watch, she realized that it had been thirty-five minutes since she'd applied the dye to her hair. She wasn't upset, though. The stuff was so old, it probably wouldn't even work. She stuck her head under the tap in the tub and started to rinse the dye out.

She rubbed her head until she couldn't feel any more gunk squishing between her fingers. Then she squeezed out the excess water and stood up to look into the mirror.

There was definitely something different about her hair—it looked lighter. She wasn't sure she'd call it red, though. It was hard to tell what color hair she now had, with her head soaking wet.

From under the sink she pulled out a blow-dryer. Plugging it in, she aimed the blast of hot air at her head. As the hot air dried her hair and the new color became clearly visible, her eyes slowly widened in horror.

She gazed at her reflection for several minutes. She'd wanted to make a dramatic change in her appearance. And this was definitely dramatic.

She went back into the bedroom. "Tasha . . ."

Tasha was still looking at the computer screen, and her back was turned to Amy.

"This is so great," Tasha said. "I found the e-mail addresses for all the big talk shows. Ricki, Jenny, Oprah, and Jerry. So I've written to them and asked if they'd help find Jeanine's parents. This is the kind of stuff they do all the time. Maybe Jeanine could be reunited with her parents on TV!" Tasha turned to Amy. "You know she'd love to . . ." She stopped short.

Amy managed a weak smile. "What do you think?"

Tasha found her voice. "You used my mother's hair dye."

"Well, she was just going to throw it away, right?"

"Right," Tasha murmured. It was clear that was not the reason why she looked disturbed.

Self-consciously Amy fingered a lock of her hair. It didn't feel any different. But when she pulled the lock around where she could see it, her stomach began to churn.

"What do you think?" she asked again.

"It's—it's different," Tasha admitted. "Not exactly like the picture on the box, though. It's more . . . orange."

"I think I'd call it dark gold," Amy said.

Tasha's head bobbed up and down. "Absolutely. It's gold. And it's *interesting*. Personally, I think it's a lot better to be interesting than just ordinary pretty."

They both heard a door slam downstairs, and Amy jumped. It couldn't be Tasha's parents—they didn't slam doors.

A few seconds later Eric bounded up the stairs and appeared in the doorway. "Hi, what's . . ." He wasn't able to finish his question with "up." He froze and stared at Amy.

Amy didn't need supersensitivity to realize that there was no admiration in his expression. Eric was clearly aghast.

"What did you do?" he cried out.

Amy tried to sound casual. "I dyed my hair. It's no big deal. I just felt like a change."

"Have you gone crazy?" Eric asked bluntly.

She touched her hair self-consciously again. "You don't like it?"

"No."

"Well, that's too bad," Amy said defiantly. "Because I do. And if you want to break up with me because you don't like my hair, then go right ahead. I don't care."

"I didn't say anything about breaking up," Eric objected.

"You're thinking it," Amy accused him. "You're thinking that you don't want to see me anymore."

"No, I'm not," Eric replied. "But you're right, I might not see you anymore. Because I'm thinking that your mother is going to kill you."

"Don't be ridiculous," Amy said loftily.

But Eric wasn't far from wrong.

six 6

"Amy! How could you do something like that!"

Amy had never seen her mother so angry. It was unnerving. She coped by acting nonchalant. "It's no big deal, Mom. It's not like I had it cut. You never said anything about not coloring it."

"But you shouldn't have done something like that without asking me first!"

Amy knew her mother was right, which made her more defensive. "I couldn't ask you! You'd just have said no!"

"Of course I'd have said no! You're much too young to be dying your hair. And it could be dangerous!"

Amy rolled her eyes. "How can hair color be dangerous?" she shouted. "Will I get split ends or something?"

"Don't you use that tone of voice with me, young lady. You know perfectly well why it could be dangerous. You're not like other people. We have no idea how certain things might affect you, how your body could respond to particular chemicals! Amy, doing something like this to yourself—you could harm yourself permanently! You could kill yourself!"

Amy hadn't considered that, and the thought sent chills down to her toes. But she refused to let her mother think she was right. "Or maybe it could turn me into a real normal person," she shot back. "Only I could never be real and normal, could I? Because I don't even have a real and normal mother."

Nancy stood very still, and Amy wondered if she'd gone too far.

She had.

When Nancy finally spoke, her voice was calm and deadly serious. "Amy, I may not be your real mother, and I may not be a normal mother. But I'm the only mother you have, and you are legally my daughter. That gives me the right to tell you that what you did was wrong. And it gives me the right to punish you. You're grounded for a week."

All her superior skills couldn't help Amy come up with a response. So she did the only thing she could think of. She turned away and stormed up the stairs to her room, where she slammed the door and threw herself on her bed.

She didn't cry. She was too angry to cry. She'd never been grounded before in her life. Of course, she'd never done anything as stupid as this in her life. Even so, she would never, never admit that she could see her mother's point of view.

Dinnertime came and went. Amy hadn't budged from her room, and Nancy hadn't come up to get her. Fortunately, Amy had a candy bar stashed in her desk drawer, so she didn't starve. But she wasn't feeling particularly full when she went to bed that night.

Maybe that was why she didn't sleep well. She didn't have any weird dreams, but she kept waking up and feeling unlike herself. The third time she woke up, she decided she was thirsty. And she didn't want water from the tap in the bathroom—she wanted the bubbly kind they kept in the refrigerator.

Tiptoeing down the stairs and into the kitchen, Amy took out a bottle of mineral water and poured some into a glass. It was very refreshing. As she drank a second glassful, her eyes went to the window that faced the street. She almost choked, and her hand tightened on the glass so she wouldn't drop it. Someone was out there. Watching her.

She'd heard about déjà vu, when a person experienced

something they were sure they'd been through before. But it had never happened to her. Now, looking at the window, she remembered a time when she'd seen someone out there, staring at her.

That time the person had turned out to be a photographer hired by the organization to find her and take pictures of her. She recalled the flash of the man's camera as he tried to photograph her from across the street in the dead of night.

This person wasn't holding a camera. Amy concentrated and focused her vision to overcome the distance and the darkness. With some effort, she could make out the figure across the street.

And she recognized her, even though the woman wasn't driving a bright blue convertible sports car. It was definitely the woman who had asked her for directions and had approached her at the mall.

The name came back to her easily. Camilla.

What was she doing out there? Why was she watching Amy? Amy didn't have the slightest idea. That last time, with the photographer, she hadn't known why he was lurking there either. She'd been afraid. . . .

Funny how she didn't feel afraid this time.

seven

"Where's Tasha?" Amy asked Eric when she found him standing alone on her doorstep the next morning.

"She left early. She wanted to use one of the fast computers in the media center." He was staring at Amy. "Didn't you wash your hair this morning?"

"Of course I washed my hair. I wash my hair every morning."

"Isn't that stuff supposed to wash out?"

"No," Amy replied shortly. "It grows out." Determined not to feel self-conscious, she'd decided to pretend this was exactly how she wanted her hair to look. She'd even worn her black jeans with a black T-shirt to go with her new look. Her orange hair was pulled back tightly in a ponytail, and she'd fixed stick-on rhinestones to her earlobes.

"Did your mother go ballistic?" Eric asked.

"I'm grounded."

"You're grounded!"

Amy nodded glumly. "For a week."

Eric looked at her in dismay. "That means you can't come to my game Friday night!"

"I can't go anywhere."

He sighed. "I guess I can't blame your mother. I mean, this is the kind of thing you expect to get grounded for."

She looked at him in annoyance. Was he actually taking her mother's side?

"At least it's only for a week," he continued. "But it's too bad you're going to miss my game. I think I play better when I know you're watching me."

Now she was getting really irritated. He wasn't just backing her mother, he was only thinking about himself. She'd planned to tell him about seeing Camilla the night before, but faced with that attitude, she didn't bother. He'd probably insist on going back and telling Nancy right that minute.

She hadn't told her mother about Camilla either. Nancy had been running around that morning, trying to get ready for some early meeting, and they'd barely spoken. And after the confrontation over her hair, Amy wasn't in the mood to share any confidences with her mother anyway.

Eric misread her silence. "You know, your hair really doesn't look all that bad," he said kindly.

"Thanks a lot," she muttered. She figured Eric was so concerned with himself and his upcoming basketball game that he probably missed the sarcasm in her voice. Personally, even though she wasn't thrilled with her hair color, she knew it was a big fad among the girls at school to use strawberry or raspberry powdered fruit drink to make a more permanent color change. She often saw girls walking around school with pink-tinged hair. Her own orange locks wouldn't look that outrageous.

"I was grounded once for a month," Eric was saying now. "I can't even remember why now. Really, a week isn't so bad."

She let him go on thinking she was upset about having orange hair and being grounded, when she really had much bigger things on her mind. Like finding out exactly who Camilla was. And why she was so interested in Amy.

Amy just couldn't believe Camilla was involved with the organization. Sure, the organization had top-notch agents. She remembered, all too well, the man her mother had dated for a while, the one who'd seemed so wonderful. Amy had really liked him. And he'd turned out to be one of them.

But Camilla had exuded warmth and sincerity. Still, Amy had to be realistic. Camilla could be an enemy. Amy didn't know what to think. So as she went into the school building, she tried not to think at all.

The hair was helpful. She got a lot of attention. Most of her classmates approved of anyone who did or wore something wild, so the majority of the comments were friendly. But she wasn't at all surprised when she reached her homeroom and Jeanine gaped in a way that was definitely not complimentary.

"Amy, what happened to you?" Jeanine said reprovingly, and loudly enough for anyone within a ten-mile radius to hear. "If you want to change your hair color, you should really go to a professional." She circled Amy, examining her hair critically. "You've got about six different shades here," she declared triumphantly. "And you missed spots."

Jeanine's little fan club erupted into a chorus of giggles. Amy ignored them. "A beauty salon is very expensive, Jeanine. Some of us don't get the kind of allowance that's lavished on you."

Now it was Amy's turn to receive support from some classmates. No one liked the way Jeanine flaunted her wealth.

Jeanine scowled. "I hope Tasha doesn't think I'm

rich. Like I said yesterday, she gets one week to find my parents." After a moment she added, "Well, maybe two. But only if she shows me she's making progress by the end of the first week. Tell her that."

"Tell her yourself," Amy said.

Jeanine gave her a hurt look. "Amy, this is a very difficult time for me." She placed a hand over her heart. "You could try to be a little more understanding and helpful." She punctuated this with a sniff, as if she was struggling to hold back a sob.

Like she was the only person in the world who had problems, Amy thought. She wondered how Jeanine would react if she heard of Amy's predicament with Camilla.

The mere thought made Amy shudder. She certainly couldn't expect any compassion from Jeanine. Instead, Jeanine would probably relish creating even more problems—really big problems—with any information that came her way. Yes, there were good reasons to keep her secrets very secret. Thank goodness she had Tasha and Eric to talk to. And her mother, of course. Well, at least she *used* to be able to talk to her mother.

It wasn't an easy day for Amy. Comments and compliments about her hair couldn't distract her from the more serious issue on her mind. In the classrooms that faced the school parking lot, she kept her eyes peeled for a glimpse of the bright blue sports car. She was reprimanded by teachers several times for not paying attention.

When she had a class in a room without a view, she came up with a variety of excuses to step out so she could take a peek into the parking lot. Teachers in those classes kept asking her if she was feeling okay.

At lunchtime Tasha wasn't at their usual table in the cafeteria. Amy found her in the media center, glued to a computer and munching a sandwich she'd brought from home. She barely acknowledged Amy's presence.

"This computer is so much faster than mine," she murmured. "I can get into a Web site in less than half a second."

"How's it going?" Amy asked.

"Okay." Tasha looked at Amy. "I heard you got grounded. That stinks."

Amy appreciated her friend's sympathy. "Yeah. It's just for a week, so I'll survive. Listen, in homeroom Jeanine was saying maybe she'll give you an extra week."

"Great, I'll need it."

Amy wasn't sure whether Tasha was referring to the extra time or the extra money. Probably both. In any case, Tasha was practically twitching with impatience to get back to her work, and Amy decided to tell her later about seeing Camilla.

But Tasha stayed at school to use the fancy computer

for the hour that the media center remained open after classes. And Eric had basketball practice. So Amy walked home alone, with ample time to ponder her situation.

Fortunately, when she turned the corner onto her street, something distracted her. A police car was parked practically in front of her house.

Her step and her heartbeat quickened at the same time. Wild notions ran through her head—maybe Camilla had tried to break into her house and a neighbor had seen her and called the police. . . .

But there was no sign of the mysterious Camilla. The Candlers' next-door neighbor, Monica Jackson, was outside talking to two police officers.

Monica was an artist, and practically every week she chose a single color and devoted herself to wearing it. This week she was in shades of violet—and that included her hair. When Monica had first moved in, Amy had thought she was a little strange, but now she was used to her. And since this was Los Angeles, where there were a lot of offbeat people, the police officers didn't seem startled by Monica's appearance at all.

Whatever had happened to Monica couldn't have been too terrible, because when she saw Amy approaching, a huge smile broke out on her face and she clapped her hands. "Amy, sweetie, I *love* your hair!"

"Thanks," Amy said. "What's going on?"

Monica's smile vanished. "I was in a little accident. Not my fault, of course."

Amy could now see Monica's banged-up old car in the driveway. It was a little—no, a *lot* more banged up than before. There was a fresh dent in the front passenger door.

"I was sideswiped by a creep in a black limo," Monica told her. "Then the creep took off. He hit and ran." She turned to the police. "That's a crime, right?"

Amy hoped the limo driver wasn't the brother of Eric's friend. But that wasn't too likely. Los Angeles was crawling with limousines.

"Can you do something to find him?" Monica pleaded with the police.

They echoed Amy's thought. "Lady, do you have any idea how many black limousines exist in Los Angeles? Now, if you'd managed to get a look at his license plate . . ."

"I did see his license plate," Monica insisted. "I just don't have a good memory. But I'm sure there was a letter J. Or maybe it was G. . . ."

The police officers were shaking their heads. "Sorry, miss." But Monica had just given Amy an idea. And unlike Monica, Amy had a very good memory.

She ran into her house, stood very still, closed her eyes tightly, and concentrated as hard as she could. Gradually the image of a bright blue sports car formed in her head. Slowly details emerged: the nameplate that showed the make of the car, the shape of the headlights, the license plate. State of California. Some letters, numbers . . . Amy whipped out a notebook and scrawled what she saw in her head.

Yes, that was Camilla's license plate number.

The phone rang. For one crazy moment Amy thought it just might be Camilla.

"Hello?"

"Hi, sweetie."

Amy tried not to let the disappointment show in her voice. "Hi, Mom."

"I just wanted to make sure everything's okay."

"Of course everything's okay."

"Well, fine. I'll be home around seven."

Amy hung up the phone with a grimace. Nancy hadn't called to see if everything was okay. She'd been checking to make sure Amy was home. Amy's mother had lost all trust in her. She was probably lying about coming home at seven o'clock. She'd be there at six just to make sure Amy hadn't sneaked out. For a moment Amy almost wished she had someplace to sneak out to.

But she wasn't going anywhere. So she knew Camilla's license plate number—she didn't have the slightest idea what to do with it. Call the police, maybe? According to the officers outside, they used this type of information to track people down. They could arrest Camilla. But for what? For spying on Amy? That wasn't what Amy wanted. She wasn't sure what she did want—but putting Camilla behind bars wasn't it.

Amy tried to keep herself busy. Making and eating a peanut butter and banana sandwich, with chocolate sprinkles, on white bread with the crusts cut off, consumed twenty minutes. Homework took up another ten. Then she turned on the television and flipped through the channels, not looking at any program for more than five minutes.

When the doorbell rang, an unusual thrill of anticipation shot through her. She jumped up to see who had dropped by. But it was just Tasha.

"Can I go online with your computer?" Tasha begged. "My mother's working out vacation plans on mine, and it could take hours."

"Okay," Amy said. They went up to her room, and Tasha sat down at Amy's desk.

"I want to see if there are any answers to my e-mails," she said.

"You can check *your* e-mail on *my* computer?" Amy asked.

"Sure. I just have to access my own server."

Amy had e-mail, but she wouldn't have known how to do that. Tasha was a real pro with computers.

"Ooh, there's a response from a talk show!" Tasha squealed. "And two others! Wow, that was fast!" But seconds later she issued a moan that clearly expressed disappointment.

"What's the matter?" Amy asked.

"They're not interested in finding Jeanine's parents."

"None of them?"

"No. Oh well, I'll just have to do it on my own." She turned to Amy with a shrug of resignation. Then her expression changed. "What's the matter with *you?*"

Amy almost smiled. This was a true best friend. No matter how much Tasha had on her own mind, she'd eventually see that something was bugging Amy.

"Something's wrong," Tasha said. "And it's not just being grounded."

So Amy told her about seeing Camilla the night before.

Tasha's immediate reaction was just like her brother's. "Amy, she must be one of *them,*" she said in a hushed and frightened tone.

Amy shook her head. "I don't think so."

"Why?"

"I don't know. I just don't think she is. But I want to find her."

"Do you know her last name?" Tasha asked.

"No. But I have her license plate number."

Tasha lit up. "You can get her full name from that! Maybe even her address and phone number!"

"How? I don't want to call the police."

"You don't have to. Did you see that article in the newspaper about the teenager who broke into the computer system at some huge corporation and gave everyone a raise?"

Amy gasped. "Are you saying you can break into the police computer system?"

"Probably not. But I bet I can find someone else who's already accessed it and put it online." Tasha started hitting keys on the computer.

"I didn't know you could do stuff like that," Amy said in awe.

"Don't tell anyone," Tasha pleaded. "I'd never do anything illegal. And I don't want anyone thinking I'm a real computer nerd."

It wasn't a simple task. Amy sat on her bed and flipped through old magazines while Tasha worked. It took Tasha half an hour to even find a lead. And it was another fifteen minutes before she let out a cry of triumph. "I think I've got it!"

Amy leaped off her bed and looked over Tasha's shoulder. Tasha typed in the letters and numbers of the license plate and hit Enter. A second later a name appeared on the screen.

Amy held back a gasp that would have been more like a scream. The first name was exactly what she'd expected: Camilla. But the last name came as a total shock.

Jaleski.

eight

"**J**aleski," Tasha read aloud, as if they both needed to hear the name to believe it was really there. "Jaleski. Amy, wasn't that the name of the doctor who—"

"Yes," Amy replied. She stared at the screen as the memories flooded back. The first time she'd come across the name had been when she read it on an official document—as a signature on her own birth certificate. But she'd soon learned that Dr. Jaleski was no ordinary doctor. James Jaleski, M.D., Ph.D., had been the director of Project Crescent. He had been her mother's boss at the laboratory back in Washington, D.C., twelve years earlier. He was the man responsible for Amy's existence. So even though Amy hadn't been born in a normal way, he was, in a sense, the doctor who'd "delivered" her.

Not long after first hearing about him, Amy had been able to attach a face to the name. Her mother had decided it was time for Amy to learn about herself, her strengths and limitations. So she had taken Amy to meet the man who knew more about her than anyone else. Amy recalled how secretive the trip had been to the little cottage on the other side of Los Angeles. Dr. Jaleski had been in hiding—from the same people who wanted Amy—and Nancy hadn't wanted to put him in any danger.

Amy had felt a bond right away with Dr. Jaleski, or Dr. J, as she came to call him. He was elderly, white-haired and retired, but he was still lively and energetic, and he had a good sense of humor. She'd felt that he really knew her, really understood her. Later she'd gone on her own to see him when she had a problem, and he'd helped her. She had looked forward to a long and close relationship with Dr. Jaleski.

But it was not to be. Soon after that second visit, Dr. Jaleski was dead.

Automatically Amy's hand went to her throat. Nestled in the curve of her collarbone was a silver pendant that hung from a chain. It was no ordinary piece of jewelry. Dr. Jaleski had made the little silver crescent moon especially for her. It was a replica of the mark on Amy's right shoulder blade, the mark that identified her as a clone. The mark would always be there. As for the pendant, she wasn't superstitious, but she believed it protected her, and she rarely took it off.

Tasha was still fooling around on the computer. "There's no address or phone listed," she was saying when Amy heard the door open and close downstairs.

"Amy?"

"I'm up here," Amy called out to her mother. She heard footsteps on the stairs.

"Quick, get out of that file," she whispered to Tasha. Amy didn't want Nancy to see the name Jaleski on the screen and start asking questions.

By the time her mother appeared at the door, the screen was blank. "Hi, Ms. Candler," Tasha chirped. "Amy was letting me use her computer."

Nancy nodded and smiled, but she said nothing, and her concerned eyes were on Amy. Tasha got the message. "I guess my mom must be putting dinner on the table. See ya tomorrow, Amy."

"Right, see ya," Amy echoed.

"But I won't come by for you in the morning," Tasha said. "I want to get to school when the media center opens so I can use the fast computer."

At least Nancy waited until Tasha was out of the house before she began scolding. "Amy, being grounded doesn't just mean staying home. It means no visitors, either."

"Well, how was I supposed to know that?" Amy asked irritably. "I've never been grounded before."

"You've never given me a reason to ground you before," her mother replied.

"So you're just making up the rules as you go along?" Amy asked accusingly. Even as she spoke, she was horrified by her own tone. She had never spoken in such an insolent way to her mother before. She could see that Nancy too was startled, and she fully expected that her punishment would be extended for another week.

But the shock faded from Nancy's face, and she just looked tired. "I have a lot of work to do tonight," she said. "I'm writing a grant proposal, and that requires a lot of research." Amy had no idea what a grant proposal was, and though she had a feeling she should show interest by asking, the anger and confusion that were still seething inside her wouldn't let her speak.

"I'll make some dinner," Nancy said. "Unfortunately, I'll have to work while I'm eating, but I'll leave yours on the kitchen counter."

"Thanks," Amy mumbled. As soon as her mother left, she dived under her bed to retrieve the latest edition of the huge Los Angeles telephone directory. She flipped rapidly through the pages till she got to the *J*'s and ran her finger down the column of listings.

Jaleron, Jalerry, Jalesh . . . Jaleski. There was only one: Jaleski, Mary. Amy knew who that was.

Mary was Dr. Jaleski's daughter. She had been living with her father when Amy met Dr. Jaleski, and she was the one who had brought Amy the silver pendant after Dr. Jaleski died.

Amy amended that thought. After Dr. Jaleski was killed. Because that was what had happened. No one had ever been accused of committing any crime. The cause of his death had been ruled a heart attack, but Amy was pretty sure the people who were watching her had found him and decided he knew too much to stay alive. The fact that he'd had an unlisted phone number at the time hadn't saved him.

Jaleski was an unusual name. Camilla had to be a relative of Mary's. Quickly Amy reached for the phone, but then she put it down. It had been a long time since she'd seen Mary, and though Mary had been friendly and kind the last time they'd met, Amy always wondered if Mary held her responsible for leading the killer to their home.

But Camilla's last name was the only clue Amy had. She picked up the phone again and punched in the numbers. Listening to the ringing, she held her breath.

Then there was a click—but it wasn't a person on the other end, it was a machine.

No name was given, but she recognized Mary's recorded voice, announcing that she was out of town and wouldn't be back until the following Tuesday, and that the caller had one minute to leave a message.

Amy didn't leave a message. There was no way she could explain in one minute why she was calling.

"Amy?" Her mother's voice floated up from downstairs. "I need to go online with my computer. Are you on the phone?"

Amy replaced the receiver. "No."

So now the phone line would be tied up. Amy couldn't do any more exploring on the Internet—even if she knew how. She understood the basics of the Internet and the Web, of course, but she didn't know how to do the extensive, complex searches Tasha was capable of carrying out.

It dawned on her that she was hungry, so she went downstairs. Her mother's office was just off the kitchen, in what used to be a pantry. The door was closed, but Amy could see a light coming through the crack at the bottom. Nancy was hard at work.

All her life, Amy had known that all she had to do was knock on the door and announce that she had a problem and Nancy would drop everything to help her.

Or at least, that was how it used to be. She wasn't so sure anymore.

At least Nancy had left dinner on the counter for her. It looked pretty good, too—cold roast beef, potato salad from her favorite deli, a fresh green salad with lots of plump red tomatoes. She took the dinner back up to her room and ate in silence. Then she brushed her teeth, put on a sleep T-shirt, and got into bed. She wasn't going to read that night—she wanted to get up particularly early the next morning, and she even reset her alarm clock to ensure that she would.

She was up, showered, and dressed a full hour earlier than usual. Her mother was at the kitchen table, and she was surprised to see Amy ready to leave so early.

"I have to do something in the school media center," Amy informed her.

Her mother didn't ask what, and Amy was convinced it was because she wasn't interested. But at least she didn't tell Amy that being grounded meant she couldn't leave the house early.

Amy's timing was perfect. Just as she closed the front door behind her, she saw Tasha emerging from her condo.

Tasha was surprised to see her. "Hi," she said, yawning. "How come you're up so early?"

"I want to go to the media center with you," Amy told her. "You can help me find out more about Camilla Jaleski."

Tasha grimaced. "Gee, Amy, I wish I could help you, but I'm hot on a trail today. You wouldn't believe what I found out last night, and I have to follow it up. There's this database I can access from the computer at school that I can't get into from home."

Amy glared at her. "You don't have time to help me, your best friend? You'd rather help rotten, nasty Jeanine Bryant?"

Tasha shrugged. "Rotten, nasty Jeanine Bryant is paying me money to get a job done, and I want to get my ears pierced."

Amy raised haughty eyebrows. "So money comes before friendship?"

Tasha grinned. "Come on, Amy, you'd do the same thing if you could get *your* ears pierced."

She had a point.

"Look, if I find out what I need before the bell, I'll help you," Tasha told Amy as they started to walk.

"Yeah, okay. Tasha, I have to find out who this woman is and why she's following me."

"There's probably a very simple explanation," Tasha said. "Maybe she's Dr. Jaleski's nosy cousin or aunt or something, and she's always believed that he was a mad scientist, like Dr. Frankenstein. Family rumors about his weird experiments have probably spread far and wide, and now she wants to see a real live human clone. You're better off keeping away from her."

"That's a little far-fetched."

Tasha shrugged. "Maybe, but wait till you hear what I found out! Have you ever heard of Sarah Travers? She's on a soap opera. Anyway, I was searching a gossip file, and there was an item from years ago, about how she gave birth to her costar's child and put the baby up for adoption. And it was on the same date as Jeanine's birthday! Right here in Los Angeles!"

Amy groaned. "I refuse to believe that Jeanine has celebrity parents. Beside, there were probably a thousand babies born that day in Los Angeles."

"But I accessed a photo of this Sarah Travers," Tasha continued. "She looks like Jeanine! Well, I guess Jeanine looks like her. They both have squinty eyes and tiny noses."

"Lots of people have squinty eyes and tiny noses," Amy said. "Especially if you include aliens." Then she remembered something else. "Besides, Jeanine wasn't even born in Los Angeles."

"She wasn't?"

"No. Don't you remember how she told everyone she was Little Miss North Carolina, or Miss North Carolina Baby Princess, or something like that, when she was six?"

Tasha's face fell. "I don't have your memory."

"Now will you help me find Camilla Jaleski?" Amy asked.

"I still want to check out another rumor I read," Tasha replied. "The main singer in one of those boy bands supposedly had an affair with a girl from a big girl band before they were famous. They might have had a baby."

Amy rolled her eyes. "They probably would have had to have been around ten years old at the time to be Jeanine's parents."

"Well, I've found some pretty weird stories about adoptions," Tasha informed her. "There was this husband and wife, they'd been married for a long time, and both of them knew they'd been adopted as babies. They wanted to find their real parents. And they discovered that they were actually brother and sister!"

"Gross," Amy commented.

"No kidding. Can you imagine me married to Eric?" Tasha shuddered. "Then I read another true story about this guy who was searching for his natural father, and he found him, but the father was in jail for armed robbery of a gas station. And the guy was the policeman who had arrested him!"

Tasha chattered on about strange adoption tales all the way to school, and Amy had to admit the stories were pretty entertaining. They certainly kept her from thinking about Camilla.

But once they got to school and Tasha logged on to the computer in the media center, Amy had nothing to do but ponder and fantasize. What if Tasha was right? What if Camilla Jaleski was nothing more than just a curious relative, snooping around and prying into Dr. Jaleski's past? Still, Amy would like to hear the woman herself admit it.

The opportunity to do just that presented itself during the last period. The dreary geography teacher was rambling on about South American exports. Half the class appeared to be sleeping, while the other half was staring out the windows. Amy was among the second half, gazing out the window at nothing in particular and wishing the time would pass faster.

Suddenly she sat up straight. Was her mind playing tricks? Was it wishful thinking, or was she really watching a bright blue sports car turn into the Parkside Middle School parking lot?

Amy closed her eyes and opened them again. The blue sports car was definitely moving slowly through the crowded lot, and as it passed directly in front of Amy's classroom, she caught a glimpse of blond hair. It was Camilla Jaleski.

Amy leaped up from her seat. The teacher frowned at her. "Amy? Do you have a question?"

"Um, could I be excused, please?" Amy asked. She was already moving toward the door as she spoke.

The teacher's frown deepened. "Class will be over in five minutes. I believe you can wait that long."

"No," Amy said. "No, I can't!" And she ran out of the room.

No one was in the hall, so Amy could move at top speed.

She burst out of a side door and looked wildly over the parking lot. The sports car was still there, idling, as if it was waiting for Amy. Knowing that her classmates and the geography teacher could see her now, Amy proceeded at normal speed. Camilla too could see Amy coming in her rearview mirror, and if she didn't want a confrontation, she could easily take off. But the car didn't budge. It remained in place as Amy arrived at the driver's side window.

"Hello," Camilla said softly.

Amy didn't bother with polite conversation. "What do you want?" she asked. "Why have you been following me?"

Camilla gestured toward the passenger seat. "Will you take a ride with me? I'd like to talk to you."

How stupid did this woman think Amy was? Like every other kid in the world, she'd been taught never to get into a car with a stranger.

"We can talk right here," Amy declared. "And I'm not getting into your car."

The woman nodded. She turned off the engine, opened the car door, and got out. Amy took a step backward, even though she wasn't afraid. She knew there was no way the slight, delicate woman could overpower her.

"Who are you?" Amy asked.

"My name is Camilla Jaleski."

"I already know that," Amy said impatiently. "But who are you? What do you want?"

A veil seemed to cover the woman's bright blue eyes. Amy had the feeling she was trying very hard to hold back tears. But she said nothing.

Amy raised her voice. "Why are you following me? Tell me or I'll make a scene and you'll have to answer to school officials and the police."

Camilla's voice trembled, and it was barely louder than a whisper. But Amy heard her loud and clear.

"Amy . . . I'm your mother."

nine

Amy had no idea how long she remained silent. It was as if the woman in front of her—Camilla Jaleski—was speaking in a foreign language. All Amy could do was stare at her without understanding.

"What did you say?" Amy finally managed to ask.

"I'm your mother, Amy. Your *birth* mother."

Again Amy went numb. It was as if all her senses had been shut off. She couldn't see. She couldn't hear. She couldn't think. She couldn't speak.

She couldn't feel a thing. She felt nothing.

Then she became dimly aware of a bell ringing, of shouting students streaming out of the school building, and of Camilla, who was starting to speak again. Amy took off.

She didn't run, but she walked with such long and furious strides that she'd almost reached her own front door before she heard the breathless voices behind her.

"Amy! Amy, wait!"

"Slow down!"

She stopped and turned. Eric was running toward her, and Tasha was about half a block behind him. Amy waited.

"What's going on?" Eric asked. His expression showed a combination of disbelief, anger, and fear. "Why were you walking like that? You were faster than a speedwalker! People were looking at you!"

She'd had no idea she'd been moving that fast. She was always so careful about not revealing her special skills in public. It had become almost second nature to walk at the rate of a normal person.

Tasha caught up. She wasn't exactly the athletic type, and her face was red from the exertion. Her voice came out in spurts. "Are—you—okay? We've been calling—and calling—to you—all the way from school! Couldn't you hear us?"

"No," Amy whispered. But she could hear perfectly well now. All her senses came rushing back—she could see, hear, think, speak . . . she could *feel*. And she burst into tears.

Eric took one arm, Tasha took the other, and together they pulled Amy into her house. "Ms. Candler?" Tasha called out.

"I don't think she's home," Eric said. "I'll call her at work."

"No!" Amy cried out. "No, don't call her!" She was gasping as she tried to control herself. Tasha and Eric exchanged worried looks.

Tasha put an arm around her. "Amy, I think you need your mother."

"My mother," Amy murmured. She started to giggle, but it came out as hiccups.

Tasha turned to her brother. "Eric, get some water."

When he returned with a tall glass, Amy took it and drank thirstily. The hiccups disappeared, and she felt calmer. "I'm okay," she said, which wasn't exactly true, but at least she no longer felt as if she was on the verge of totally losing control.

"I was just outside the gym when I saw you in the parking lot," Eric told her. "You were talking to that woman we saw at the mall."

"I saw her too," Tasha said. "But by the time I got outside, you were gone."

Amy nodded.

"What did she want?" Eric asked. His face darkened. "Did she threaten you?"

"No." Amy took a deep breath. "She just wanted to tell me she's my mother."

There was a moment of silence. "Could you say that again?" Tasha asked carefully.

"She says she's my mother," Amy said. "My natural, birth mother."

Tasha eyes widened. "Are you serious? She really said that?"

"She's a wacko? A total wacko?" Eric asked.

Amy didn't know what to say.

"She has to be nuts, Amy," Eric went on. "What she said isn't possible!"

"I know that," Amy said.

Eric turned to Tasha. "I think we should call the police."

"No!"

Tasha and Eric were taken aback. Amy herself was startled by how strong her response was. She continued more quietly.

"No, I don't want to call the police. I don't think she's dangerous, and maybe . . ."

"And maybe what?" Eric asked.

Tasha guessed what Amy was trying to say. "And maybe she's telling the truth."

Eric stared at his sister. "Now *you're* talking like a

wacko." He turned to Amy and spoke slowly and patiently, as if he was trying to explain something to a child. "Amy, listen to me. You don't have a natural mother. No one gave birth to you. You are a clone. You were created in a laboratory."

"I know how I was born, Eric," Amy said.

"Then why don't you want me to call the police?"

"I don't know." Amy stood up and moved around the living room restlessly. "You know, sometimes I wonder if my mother told me the complete truth about myself."

"That's what I'm thinking," Tasha said. "Your mother could have made up the whole story, just to explain how she got you! Or maybe you were switched at birth, like the girl on the news last week. Did you see that? She got the wrong name tag fifteen years ago when she was born, and she just found out because her real mother tracked her down! Maybe that's what Camilla has done!"

"Yeah, right." Eric snorted. "The whole clone story is a fairy tale. Then how do you explain Amy's powers? You think Camilla is Wonder Woman? Or Mrs. Superman?"

"Or Mrs. Jaleski," Amy said. "That's her last name, Eric. Camilla Jaleski."

"She could simply be a relative," Tasha reminded her.

Amy nodded. "But she could have been his wife. You know how I had this special feeling about Dr. J."

"That's just because he created you," Eric said.

"Yes," Amy replied. "But maybe in a different way than I always thought."

Tasha was nodding. Eric looked at both of them and groaned.

"You're both wacko." He got up. "I have to get ready for my game tonight. You sure you're okay?"

Amy nodded.

"I'll stay with you," Tasha offered.

"You need to find Jeanine's parents so you can get your ears pierced," Amy reminded her.

Tasha spoke solemnly. "Amy, you know I'd give up earrings for my best friend."

"Even solid gold loops?" Amy smiled and gave her friend a hug. "Really, you can go. Actually, you have to go. Nancy could be home any minute, and I'm not supposed to have company."

Amy followed Eric and Tasha to the door. "Good luck in the game," she told Eric. "I'm sorry I can't be there."

"Me too," he said. "I'll call you when I get home."

Tasha paused before stepping outside and looked at Amy curiously. "That's funny," she said.

"What's funny?" Amy asked. "Tell me the joke."

"Not funny ha-ha, funny strange. When you talk about your mother, you always call her Mom."

"Yeah, so?"

"Just now, you called her Nancy."

Amy just shrugged. "Call me later," she said, and shut the door. She went into the kitchen and considered making a peanut butter, banana, and chocolate sprinkle sandwich, but it didn't seem worth the effort, so she settled for a plain banana.

She was only halfway through peeling it when she heard her mother come in the door. For a moment Amy worried that Nancy might have seen Eric and Tasha leave. But the smile on her mother's face let her know she wasn't in any additional trouble.

"Hi, sweetie, have a nice day?"

"It was okay," Amy said. "How was your day?"

"Excellent!" her mother declared. "I made it through the first round!"

"Huh?"

"I have to go through three rounds of interviews for this promotion," Nancy explained. "On the department, college, and university levels. And I got the okay from the department interview committee today!"

"That's good," Amy said. "Congratulations. Want some banana?"

Her mother broke off a chunk and popped it into her mouth. "And, sweetie, I promise you, when this process is over, things will be different, whether I get the promotion or not." She went on to explain that she wouldn't be so busy, and that she wanted them to take a little vacation together.

Amy nodded and smiled and murmured in agreement, but she wasn't really listening. Her thoughts were a million miles away, but she couldn't say exactly where.

The phone rang, and Nancy reached for it. "Hello?" Then she frowned and replaced the receiver.

"Who was it?"

"I don't know. Whoever it was hung up." Nancy stretched and yawned. "Amy, would you mind if I just put a frozen pizza in the microwave? I'm too tired to cook, and I want to get to bed early tonight. I've got another round of interviews tomorrow."

"Sure, okay," Amy said. As far as she was concerned, her mother could have been offering frozen antelope. Dinner just wasn't a priority.

The phone rang again while they were eating. Again Nancy answered, and again there was no one at the other end of the line. Amy was helping put dishes into the dishwasher when another call came.

"Hello?" Nancy asked. Her lips tightened, and she said, "Hello," again. Then she slammed the phone down. "Amy, could one of your friends be playing games?"

"Why are you accusing my friends?" Amy asked.

"I'm not accusing anyone," her mother said. "I'm

just wondering why the person on the other end hangs up when *I* answer." She popped the last fork into the dishwasher and yawned. "I'm going to have a quick shower before I collapse." She left Amy in the kitchen and went upstairs.

Amy sat back down at the kitchen table and looked at the phone. She too was wondering who was calling, who was hanging up when Nancy answered. She had a thought and went to the phone.

Remembering a phone company commercial in which someone punched in a set of numbers to find out who the last caller had been, Amy hit the same numbers. Bingo!

The phone rang and someone answered. Amy instantly recognized the voice. "Are you trying to call me?" She didn't have to identify herself—the woman on the other end recognized her voice too.

"Yes," Camilla said. "Amy, I want to talk to you. I want to explain. Please give me a chance to tell you what I know. Will you meet me?"

Amy's grip on the receiver tightened. "Where?"

"I've been calling on my mobile phone from a bus stop. It's close to where you live." She told Amy the street corner. "Or I could come pick you up."

"No," Amy said. She looked at the clock. Nancy was in the shower, and it would take her a while to get to sleep.

"I'll be there at ten-thirty," Amy said. Then she hung up the phone, before she could change her mind.

But at ten-fifteen, she still wasn't sure she should meet Camilla. Nancy was sound asleep, so that wasn't a problem. But what was Amy getting herself into? Camilla Jaleski couldn't be her mother. But then who was she? What was her relation to Dr. Jaleski? And why did she think she could be Amy's mother? Was it like Eric had said—was she just a crazy person? Amy had to know. And it wasn't as if she couldn't protect herself if the woman did turn out to be nuts. Still, if Nancy woke up and discovered that Amy had gone out of the house . . .

The phone rang. Amy grabbed it, half hoping it was Camilla calling to cancel their meeting. But it was only Eric.

"We won!" he declared. "We murdered them, sixty-two to forty-five!"

"That's great," she whispered. "Listen, Eric, I'm really tired. Tell me all about it tomorrow, okay?"

She could tell he was disappointed, but he didn't push her. "Yeah, sure. Good night."

Carefully, quietly, she replaced the receiver. Then she picked up a light sweater, which she tied around her shoulders, crept silently downstairs, and went out the door.

It was a five-minute walk to the corner where the bus stop stood. At first, as she approached, she didn't see anyone, and she was almost relieved. Then she detected a slight movement in the shadows on the bench, and she knew it had to be Camilla.

In the darkness of the bus shelter, Camilla seemed even more fragile and delicate than before. Her blond hair framed her face like a halo. She smiled when she saw Amy, and she looked even more like an angel.

"Hello, Amy."

"Hi." Amy eyed her warily. She sat down on the other end of the bench.

"Thank you for coming," Camilla said. "By the way, I want to tell you, I like your new hair color. When I was your age, I dyed my hair purple."

"Really?" Amy murmured.

"I know this can't be easy for you," Camilla said. "It's hard for me, too. I've been searching for you for so long, Amy. And now that I've found you, I want to wrap my arms around you and hold you tight and never let you go."

Amy edged even closer to the other end of the bench. "Wait a minute," she began uneasily. She was startled when Camilla laughed lightly.

"Am I frightening you? I'm sorry, Amy. You know, that's not really your name. I mean, it's not the name I gave you when you were born. Your name is—"

"Just call me Amy, okay?" Amy interrupted.

"All right. Will you listen to my story, Amy?"

"Go ahead."

"It's your story too," Camilla said. "It's *our* story. I've been waiting twelve years to tell it to you." Amy could hear joy in her voice. The night was warm, but she shivered as Camilla began to tell her tale.

"Dr. Jaleski was my husband. When James and I married, thirteen years ago in Washington, D.C., I was much younger than he was. He had been divorced from his first wife for many years, and she had custody of their daughter."

"Mary," Amy murmured.

"Yes. Mary. I only met her once, when she was just a little older than you are now. Her mother rarely allowed her to visit. Your father was alone, and he was lonely. I wanted to give him children, lots of children." Her voice became sad. "But it was not to be. I just couldn't seem to become pregnant."

Amy tried to sound casual. "So you adopted me?" She figured she'd better play along for the time being.

"Oh, no, darling. I am your natural mother."

"But you just said you couldn't become pregnant."

"I saw many doctors, specialists," Camilla continued. "And of course, your father was one of the world's foremost scientists."

"My father?" Amy blurted out.

"Yes, darling, of course. James Jaleski is . . . *was* your father."

Amy thought back to her meetings with Dr. Jaleski. She and the doctor *had* had a special relationship—but why wouldn't he have told her he was her father? It didn't make any sense. This couldn't be true.

"I was given some medication to help me become pregnant," Camilla went on. "Experimental drugs. They weren't widely available." She gave a laugh, but it wasn't a happy one. "It's ironic, in a way. I was only able to get these drugs because of your father's connections in the scientific and medical community."

Amy shifted uncomfortably on the hard bench. It was so weird, hearing the words *your father.*

"And I did become pregnant! We were so happy, James and I. I had to continue taking the drugs so that I wouldn't lose you. And I didn't like having to do that. But I would have done anything to have you." Her voice became even softer with reminiscence. "We knew you would be a girl. We painted the nursery pink and white. . . ." Her voice drifted off for a moment. Amy waited.

"Then you were born," Camilla said, and suddenly her voice became harder. "You were beautiful and absolutely perfect. But you were . . . special."

"How do you mean, *special?*" Amy asked.

Camilla didn't exactly answer that. "The medication I had to take . . . it made you different. Special. But I didn't care. I loved you so much, Laura."

Amy took a sharp breath.

"I mean Amy," Camilla said quickly. "I wanted to treat you like any ordinary child, to raise you in a happy, normal home. But your father had other ideas."

"What other ideas?" Amy asked.

Camilla's voice became bitter. "He wanted to *use* you. He wanted to take our extraordinary baby and use her for his horrible experiments. He was greedy, Amy. He wanted more babies just like you."

"He wanted to clone me," Amy said.

"Yes. But I didn't want him to. I refused to give permission. I wouldn't let him touch you!" There was a catch in her voice, as if she was about to break down into tears, and she stopped speaking.

"What happened next?" Amy prompted her.

"He divorced me," Camilla said simply. "He kicked me out, just got rid of me. And then he sued for full custody of you." Now there was no mistaking her anger. "He made up some ridiculous story, accusing me of child abuse and neglect. He got his scientific and medical pals, with their fancy degrees and titles, to back him up. I didn't have any important friends, Amy. There was no one to stand up for me. So I lost you. And he got to do what he wanted to do."

"Make the other Amys," Amy whispered.

"Yes."

Amy felt dizzy. She put a hand on the bench to steady herself.

"I was told to keep away from you," Camilla said. "They made me leave. They said if I tried to find you, if I ever tried to get near you, I'd be arrested, and declared insane, and locked away forever. So I stayed away."

She fell silent again. This time Amy didn't prompt her to keep talking. Camilla was crying now. She didn't make any noise, but Amy could see the rivers of tears running down her cheeks.

Amy waited. She knew that Camilla would tell her more when she felt ready.

And she did.

"I was a coward," Camilla admitted. "I was afraid to fight them, to fight for you. And if you want to hate me for that, I'll understand."

"I don't hate you," Amy said spontaneously.

Now she could see a small smile forming on Camilla's face. "Thank you, darling," Camilla said humbly.

"I didn't say I *believe* you," Amy added hastily.

"I understand," Camilla said. "It's a strange story, isn't it?"

Not any stranger than the story Nancy had told her about her birth, Amy thought, but she kept that to herself.

"When I read that James had died," Camilla continued, "I wasn't so frightened anymore. I was determined to find you, to let you know who I am. The newspaper said he died in Los Angeles, so I thought there was a chance you could be here."

"Los Angeles is a big city," Amy said carefully. "How did you find me?"

"On the Internet, months ago, I found a clue. A girl named Amy was looking for other girls her age named Amy."

Amy nodded. She remembered doing that, just after learning about herself. She'd been trying to find her fellow clones.

"I knew he had called his experiment Amy," Camilla said. "He never liked the name Laura."

The dizzy feeling hadn't gone away, and now Amy was feeling a little sick. "I have to go now," she blurted out.

Camilla didn't try to force her to stay. "I understand," she said. "I just have one question."

"What?"

"That woman who took you, Nancy Candler . . . is she good to you?"

"Yes," Amy said. "Excuse me, I have to go!" And without taking another look at the woman on the bench, she ran off into the night.

ten 10

Amy lay in bed on Saturday morning, her eyes focused on a crack in the ceiling. The crack had been there forever, or at least as long as she could remember. As a child, she would imagine that it had the shape of a rabbit. A specific memory came back to her. She couldn't have been more than four when Nancy sat on the edge of her bed and read to her the story of Madeline, the little Parisian girl who had her appendix taken out in a hospital. In the story, Madeline looked at a crack in the ceiling of her hospital room and thought it looked like a rabbit. Amy's mother pointed out the crack on Amy's ceiling, and together they marveled at the coincidence.

Her mother . . . of course, Amy still associated Nancy with that word. Who else would she think of? Certainly not Camilla with her crazy story.

After leaving Camilla at the bus shelter, Amy ran all the way home at top speed. She felt safe doing that in the darkness. No one could see her. These abilities of hers, to move faster than others, to see better and hear better—there was no way they could be the result of some medication for pregnant women. If that had been true, and even if the drug had only been experimental, every pregnant woman in the world would have been clamoring to take it. Who wouldn't want to have a child who could do everything better than other children?

Thank heavens Nancy was a sound sleeper. Amy had no problem sneaking into the house and up the stairs to her room. *She* didn't sleep very soundly, though. She had strange, restless dreams, and she woke up after each dream.

They were nothing like her old nightmare of being trapped under glass while a fire raged around her. In these dreams, she saw Dr. Jaleski . . . only he didn't look like Dr. Jaleski. He had the face of a stranger. Which was interesting, because if Camilla had been speaking the truth about Dr. Jaleski, he certainly wasn't the man Amy had thought he was.

But Camilla couldn't have been speaking the truth,

because the story was just too bizarre. On the other hand, that was exactly what Amy had thought when she'd first heard Nancy's story about her origin.

What would someone else think? There weren't many people Amy could talk to. She picked up the phone and dialed.

Eric answered right away, and he sounded pleased to hear from her. "I'm sorry I woke you last night," he apologized. "I went out for pizza with the guys to celebrate the victory, and I didn't realize how late it was."

"That's okay, it wasn't so late," Amy said. "I was just feeling kind of wiped out."

"I don't blame you," Eric said. "You had a creepy experience yesterday. You know, Amy, the more I think about that Camilla woman, the more I keep thinking we should call the police."

"She doesn't want to hurt me, Eric," Amy began, but Eric didn't let her continue.

"Maybe not, but I've heard about stalkers. They don't always think they're going to hurt their victims, but sometimes they do. Remember that movie star who was killed by some maniac who said he was in love with her? Then he killed himself so they could be together in heaven. These people aren't normal."

"Neither am I," Amy reminded him. "But listen, Eric—"

"At least let's tell your mother about her," Eric suggested.

"No! I—I don't want her to start worrying. She's got too much other stuff on her mind."

Eric sighed. "Okay, but I wish you'd change your mind. Look, I gotta run. The coach wants to meet with the team to go over what we did right last night. Guess he's hoping for a repeat performance. You wanna talk to Tasha?"

"Yeah."

She heard him bellow, "Tasha, Amy's on the phone!"

Tasha came on the line. "Hi, what's up?"

"Wait a second," Amy said. She could hear her mother downstairs, moving around. She went to her door and closed it gently. Even though she felt very sure her mother couldn't hear anything, she spoke to Tasha in a whisper. "I want to tell you what happened last night," she began.

Tasha didn't interrupt. There was total silence on the other end of the line as Amy related her adventure of the night before and Camilla's strange story. When she had finished, all Tasha could do was gasp.

"Amy . . . do you think it could be true?"

"No, of course not," Amy said.

"But why would she make up a story like that?"

"I don't know, but . . ." Amy stopped suddenly. She

thought she heard a click on the phone. "Hello? Is someone else on the line?"

"Oh, I'm sorry, sweetie." It was Nancy's voice. "I didn't realize you were on the phone. Let me know when you're off, okay? I need to make a call." There was another click, which told Amy that Nancy had hung up.

"Tasha, I'll call you back later," Amy said. She hung up the phone and ran downstairs. "I'm off the phone, Mom."

"Thanks." Her mother picked up the kitchen extension and dialed. "It's busy," she murmured, and hung up.

Amy was looking out the window at the gray sky. "Mom, when is my week of being grounded over? Is it Wednesday?"

Nancy joined her at the window and put a hand on her shoulder. "I suppose I should give you time off for good behavior."

Amy winced, knowing her mother wouldn't have said that if she'd known what Amy had done the night before.

"And I know it was hard for you not to go to Eric's game," her mother continued. "How about this? Let's say that as of tomorrow morning you're free."

"Thanks," Amy said.

Nancy went back to the phone and dialed again. "Still busy," she sighed.

"Mom?"

"What?"

"When I was created, with all the other Amys, what was the pattern? I mean, who did we come from?"

"I don't understand what you're asking," Nancy said.

"I know we're considered clones, but we had to have been cloned *from* someone, right?"

Nancy stared at her. Just then the phone rang, and she picked it up. "Hello? Oh, hi, I've been trying to reach you. Do you have those papers in your office? Yes, fine. No, I'll come by today and pick them up. Bye."

She hung up the phone. "I'm sorry, Amy, what were you asking me?"

"Well, it's like the sheep clone. There was an original sheep that provided the DNA for the clone, Dolly, right? So who was the original source for us?"

"I explained that to you before," Nancy said.

"I guess I forgot," Amy lied. "Could you explain it to me again?"

"Cells were collected from a large number of people who were considered superior in specific ways," Nancy told her. "The DNA from these cells was extracted and configured in an attempt to duplicate a specific talent or ability. The cells were grown and divided. . . ." She went on with her description of the process. Amy had heard it all before.

"So there was no original," Nancy finished. "Unless you count the hundred or more people whose cells were used. But only a small part of each person contributed to making the Amys, so I wouldn't call any of them a pattern."

"Sounds complicated," Amy remarked.

"I'm sure it was," her mother said.

"What do you mean, you're sure it was? Weren't you there?"

"Not at the very beginning of the project," Nancy told her. "I was hired in the second month, after the cells were harvested."

"I see," Amy said thoughtfully. "But there were twelve identical clones that grew at the same pace?"

"That's right." Her mother hesitated. "Well, originally, there were thirteen."

"Thirteen!"

"Yes. One of the organisms was defective."

"So it was destroyed?" Amy asked.

"Actually, I'm not sure," Nancy said. She moved over to the window. "Is something wrong, Amy? You haven't asked me questions like this in a long time."

"I'm just curious," Amy said lightly. "And bored. I have to stay inside all day today, remember?"

Nancy laughed. "It's not a bad day for staying inside,"

she noted, pointing out the dark clouds that hovered overhead. "I wish *I* could. I have my last round of interviews at the university."

"At least you've got something to do," Amy grumbled.

"You can read," Nancy pointed out. "Or watch TV, or play on your computer. You just can't go out or have any company."

"I know, I know," Amy said. "Can I make a phone call now or are you going online?"

"No, go ahead and make your call," Nancy said. "Just don't stay on too long, okay?" She went into her office and shut the door.

Amy went back upstairs to her room. The call she needed to make wouldn't take much time at all. No more than a minute.

She knew Mary Jaleski was out of town until Tuesday. But lots of people who traveled called their home phones to get their messages. Maybe Mary would do that. Amy wanted some answers, and the sooner the better.

She would have only a minute to make her request, so she wanted to prepare it carefully. It had to sound right, too. Nothing too urgent. She didn't want Mary to suspect her real motives for calling. She had to say the right thing, with the right attitude.

Taking a pad and pen from a drawer, she sat down at

her desk to write out the message she would leave on Mary's answering machine.

Hello, Mary, this is Amy Candler. I was thinking about you yesterday, because I met a woman named Camilla Jaleski, and I was wondering if you were related to her.

She read that over and shook her head. No, that wasn't right. If Amy said she had met Camilla, Mary would wonder why she hadn't simply asked Camilla if she was related to Mary. She started again.

Hello, Mary, this is Amy Candler. I was thinking about you yesterday, because I met a woman named Camilla Jaleski, and she says she's related to you. Is that true?

No, she couldn't say that. It sounded too suspicious. She gave her approach more thought.

After a few minutes she began to write again.

Hello, Mary, this is Amy Candler. I was just thinking about you. I'm doing some volunteer work for . . .

She paused to think of something that would sound legitimate. It would have been useful at that moment to be able to consult Tasha, with her creative imagination. But Amy wasn't totally lacking in creativity.

I'm doing some volunteer work for the Children's Orchestra of Los Angeles. It's a fund-raising campaign, and I have to call a bunch of people. One of the people on my list is named Camilla Jaleski, and I wondered if she was any relation to you.

Yes, that was an excellent approach. That way she wouldn't have to admit to having met Camilla. And it gave her a real excuse for calling Mary. She could say that she was hoping Camilla would donate money if she knew Amy was a friend of Mary's.

Perfect. Amy refined the message, and then she timed it to make sure she could say it all in less than a minute. She just hoped there wasn't a real Children's Orchestra of Los Angeles and that if there was, Mary didn't know all about it.

As she dialed, she practiced speaking in a light and casual tone. Mary's phone began to ring, and Amy held the paper in front of her so that she could start reading immediately after the tone.

It was a total shock when the phone was answered by an actual human voice.

"Hello?"

Amy almost dropped the paper she was holding, and she couldn't speak.

"Hello?" Mary asked again.

Amy tried to keep her voice from shaking. "Hello, Mary, this is Amy Candler."

"Amy, hello! What a pleasant surprise. How are you?"

"I'm fine. How are you?"

"Fine. I was out of town on business, and I got back today, earlier than I expected. In fact, I just walked in the door. What can I do for you?"

There was a pause. Mary was waiting for Amy to state her reason for calling.

"I'm calling because, because . . . have you ever heard of someone named Camilla Jaleski?" Amy blurted out.

There was a moment of silence before Mary spoke. "Camilla Jaleski," she said softly. "Good heavens. It's been a long time since I heard that name."

"Do you know her?"

"Yes. She was my father's second wife. They weren't married very long, and I only met her once. I was living out here with my mother at the time. I rarely saw my father in those days, and I didn't talk to him much. Why are you asking about Camilla Jaleski?"

Now was the time for Amy to launch into her Children's Orchestra story, and she did. Mary seemed to buy it.

"Well, I don't think using my name will encourage her to donate money," Mary told her. "Like I said, we only met once." Her voice changed. "Amy, is this legal? I thought children couldn't be used by organizations for fund-raising activities."

"This is a special situation," Amy said quickly. "It was nice talking to you, Mary. Bye!" She hung up the phone.

It had been rude of her to end the conversation so abruptly. She should have asked Mary about her life, what she was doing, that sort of thing. Maybe talk about how much she missed Mary's father . . . who was maybe Amy's father too.

Amy fell onto her bed and tried to straighten out her thoughts. So Camilla was telling the truth, at least the part about being married to Dr. Jaleski. Mary hadn't mentioned anything about their having children, though. But if Mary and Camilla had met only once, and they were living at opposite ends of the country, maybe Mary didn't even know. . . .

Amy's breath came out in a rush. Mary didn't know she had a half sister. Amy.

She felt as if her head would explode from all the thoughts, the rush of emotions that filled her. Was this all really, truly possible? Her whole concept of herself, her knowledge of who she was—was it all wrong?

"Amy! You look upset."

Nancy stood in Amy's doorway, looking very concerned. Amy realized that her hands were on her head, in the position of someone who had a raging headache. Amy never had headaches.

"It's nothing," she said quickly. "I was just thinking."

Her mother's expression remained worried. "Are you feeling all right?"

"Of course!" Amy said brightly. "I always feel all right."

Still Nancy hesitated. "I'm going to the university now . . . but I can stay here if you need me."

"I'm fine," Amy insisted. "Honestly. *Mom*." She added that last word almost as an afterthought. For the first time in her life, it sounded strange.

But she must have been convincing, because Nancy left. Amy was then free to curl up on her bed.

It was so unreal, but everything seemed to be falling into place. Amy had a mother and a father, like other people. A sister, even. As for her unusual skills, medications taken by Camilla could certainly have enhanced her natural abilities. Teachers were always telling them that drugs could have side effects no one knew about.

Something else hit her. She wasn't one of twelve—she was an original! The other Amys she had seen and met—they were replicas of *her*.

The thought was so overwhelming that it took a moment before the ringing of the doorbell registered. She ran downstairs and found Tasha at the door.

Her friend was pale with excitement. "I just saw your mother leave," she said. "And I have to show you something." Tasha was clutching a paper tightly in her hand. "I printed this out from my computer," she said in a breathless rush. "I figured out how to get into the Washington, D.C., registry of births. Look!"

Amy took the paper. It wasn't an excellent copy, but it was completely legible and it looked very official. Across the top, ornate letters proclaimed that this was an official birth certificate, issued in the District of Columbia twelve years earlier. There was the name of a father: James Jaleski, M.D., Ph.D. And the name of a mother: Camilla Louise Jaleski. The baby was fourteen inches long, and she weighed six pounds, two ounces. Her name was Laura Jean Jaleski.

Amy started to shake.

Suddenly the door opened, and Nancy strode in. "I forgot my office keys," she was saying, and then she saw Tasha. Her lips tightened.

"I was just leaving," Tasha declared, and ran out of the house. Nancy glared at Amy, who shoved the piece of paper into the back pocket of her jeans.

"She only came over for a minute," Amy began, but Nancy wasn't in the mood for excuses.

"Amy, I said no company!" she yelled. "I can't believe this! And after I just gave you time off for good behavior!"

Amy raged right back. "You make it sound like I'm in jail! What are you, the prison warden?"

"No, I'm your mother and you are supposed to obey me!"

"Oh, really?" Amy asked her. "Says who?"

Nancy gasped at the harshness of Amy's tone. "You go to your room right now, young lady! You're grounded for another week!"

Amy turned around and stormed up the stairs, slamming her bedroom door. She took the birth certificate out of her jeans pocket and smoothed out the crumpled paper. She looked it over again.

It was all there, in black and white. The truth.

She heard the front door close downstairs, and she went to the window. Nancy was heading to the driveway. Even from this distance, Amy could see that her face was white, no doubt from distress and fury.

Amy threw herself on her bed and tried to figure out what she should do next. Call Mary Jaleski? Wait till Nancy got home and confront her with the paper?

Then the phone rang.

"Hello?"

"Hello, Amy." Camilla's voice was soft and warm.

"Hello," Amy said again.

"I was just wondering if you'd had an opportunity to think about what I told you last night."

"Yes," Amy said. "I've been thinking a lot." And then she knew what to do. "Where are you?" she asked Camilla.

"Not far from your home," Camilla replied.

"Could you come get me?" Amy asked.

She could hear Camilla draw in her breath. And when the woman spoke, Amy could hear joy in her voice.

"Oh, yes, I'll be right there!"

"Give me ten minutes," Amy said quickly. "I have to pack a few things. And—and leave a note."

"Yes," Camilla said. "Yes, that's the right thing to do. I'll be over in ten minutes."

Amy hung up and got her overnight case from the closet. She tossed in some underwear, a couple of T-shirts, a nightgown, and another pair of jeans, and ran into the bathroom and got her toothbrush.

Then she sat down at her desk and wrote.

Dear Mom,

She ripped the paper off the pad, crumpled it, and threw it in her wastebasket. She started again.

Dear Nancy,
I found out who I am. I'm going to my real mother.

She hesitated over the closing. *Love? Sincerely?* Finally she just wrote *Amy*.

Had it been ten minutes yet? She went to her window and looked out.

The bright blue sports car was right across the street. Amy wasn't surprised to see that the top was up. It had started to rain. Clearly, this woman wasn't crazy.

Amy picked up her suitcase and the backpack that held her schoolbooks. She stopped and stuck the note in the frame of the hanging mirror.

eleven

Amy stood on the terrace of Camilla's apartment and looked out over the many Los Angeles neighborhoods that spread out before her. This was a very different view than the one from Parkside, where Amy had grown up. Instead of a suburban setting with private homes, Camilla lived in a congested part of the city where office buildings and high-rise apartments sprouted everywhere.

Camilla's own apartment was on the twentieth floor. The apartment wasn't fancy, and though the simple furniture was tasteful, it didn't look especially comfortable. So while Camilla went off to fix tea, Amy ventured through the sliding doors onto the terrace.

After taking in the view, Amy imagined it could be very pleasant to eat dinner out here on nice evenings, on the little table with its two chairs. She leaned over the railing, trying to see if there was a sign that would tell her the name of the street. Focusing intently, she made out that they were on Starling Road.

A voice from behind startled her. "Laura! Laura! Don't do that!"

Amy turned. Camilla was pale.

"You frightened me, hanging over the railing like that!"

"I was just looking around," Amy said. "Don't worry, I won't fall."

A bit of color returned to Camilla's face. She set a tray down on the little table. "I'm sorry for yelling like that," she said. "But it means so much to me, having you here. And if anything happened to you again, I couldn't bear it. Come, sit down with me."

Taking a seat at the table, Amy wondered what Camilla meant by anything happening to her again. She must be referring to the fact that Dr. Jaleski had taken Amy away from her.

"I met my father once, you know," Amy told Camilla as she held out her cup for tea. "Twice, actually. Of course, I didn't know he was my father then."

Camilla smiled as she poured tea from a china pot into Amy's cup, but she didn't say anything.

"I know he was a very important scientist," Amy continued. "But I'm surprised that he wanted to clone his own daughter. I guess when he saw how, well, different I was, he couldn't resist the opportunity. How did you know I was special when I was born?"

"You were perfect," Camilla said simply.

"Well, yeah, I know that," Amy said, and then she felt a little embarrassed, talking about herself being perfect. But this was her mother. She should be able to say anything in front of her and not worry about sounding conceited.

"But how could you tell I was exceptional?" she asked. "Did I do something other babies couldn't do? Did I *look* different?"

"Drink your tea before it gets cold," Camilla said.

Amy took a sip. It was sweet and minty. "Mmm, it's good."

Camilla gazed at her fondly. "I'm glad you like it." She reached across the table and took Amy's hand. Her eyes were shining. "I still can't believe you're here, sitting across the table from me."

Amy smiled back. "It's nice to be here."

Camilla's tinkling laugh filled the air. "Don't worry, Amy, I'm not going to start acting all mushy and sentimental. Have a sandwich."

Amy took one of the little triangles of bread off the tray. But after one bite she put it down.

Camilla seemed concerned. "What's the matter? Don't you like it?"

Amy was embarrassed again. "It's kind of fishy."

"That's smoked salmon, a delicacy. But if you don't like it . . ." Camilla got up and disappeared into the apartment. Amy hoped she wasn't looking for something else for her to eat. She wasn't even hungry.

But when Camilla returned, she was only carrying a pad and a pencil. She sat back down at the table. "No smoked salmon," she said aloud as she wrote. "I will never buy smoked salmon again. Do you like egg salad? Try one of the brown-bread sandwiches."

Amy wasn't particularly crazy about egg salad either, but she could swallow that a lot easier than salmon, so she took one. She thought it was awfully nice of Camilla to be so concerned about what she liked and didn't like.

"You don't like smoked salmon," Camilla murmured again, almost in wonderment. "There's so much I have to learn about you, Laura. Oh, I'm sorry, I really should call you Amy. That's the name you grew up with and it's the name you're used to hearing. It's just that I've spent so many years thinking of you as Laura."

"Laura," Amy echoed. It wasn't one of her favorite names, but it wasn't terrible. At least she hadn't been called Heather. Impulsively she leaned toward Camilla. "You can call me Laura if you want to."

"That would make me very happy," Camilla said. "Would you like to know why I gave you that name?"

"Sure, okay."

Camilla's voice became dreamy. "There's a wonderful movie called *Laura*. It was made a long time ago, in the 1940s, I think. I saw it on television, just before you were born. . . ." Her voice drifted away, and her eyes became cloudy, as if she was seeing the movie in her mind.

"What was it about?" Amy asked her.

Camilla's eyes cleared. "It was a mystery. A detective is investigating the death of a woman named Laura. He looks at the portrait of Laura in her apartment, and he falls in love with it. But it turns out that the woman who was killed wasn't Laura after all. Laura is alive. . . ."

"So the movie has a happy ending?"

Camilla gazed at her. "Yes, a very happy ending." Her gaze was so intense, Amy felt almost uncomfortable. But it didn't last. Camilla took a gulp of her tea and smiled brightly.

"Now, what would you like to do today?"

Amy didn't know what to suggest.

"Do you like shopping?" Camilla asked her.

"I love shopping," Amy confessed.

Camilla's laugh filled the air again. "Then you inherited that from me! Let's go to Rodeo Drive."

"Rodeo Drive?" Amy echoed in awe. She knew about

the famous, expensive area in Beverly Hills, but she'd never shopped there.

It turned out that Camilla was very much at home on Rodeo Drive. She knew every store, and in some of the stores, the people knew her. "Good afternoon, Mrs. Jaleski," a salesperson would say.

"Hello!" Camilla would call out gaily. "This is my daughter, Laura."

The salesperson always looked a little surprised, and he or she would say something like "I didn't know you had a daughter!" Then Amy-Laura would be treated very nicely, much better than any salesperson at the mall ever treated her.

It wasn't long before Amy realized she could have anything she wanted. Every time she admired something—a skirt, a necklace, a pair of shoes—Camilla asked her if she wanted it. And Amy was tempted.

But something made her say, "No, thank you," over and over again. Whenever Nancy offered to buy her something she liked, she always accepted it. But she couldn't accept gifts from strangers. Of course, Camilla wasn't a stranger, but Amy wasn't ready to think of her as her mother. Not yet.

When they passed a hair salon, Amy paused to gaze at the pictures in the window. She caught sight of her reflection and saw that her orange hair looked glaringly bright.

"Do you really think my hair is nice like this?" she asked Camilla.

"Absolutely," Camilla assured her. "It's marvelous. But if you want to change the color, you can. Or you can have a haircut, if you like."

A haircut! *This* she might actually accept.

But when they went into the salon, there were no appointments available for that afternoon. "The next available appointment is on Monday at ten-thirty," the receptionist told Camilla.

"There are other salons," Camilla said, but Amy didn't see any as they proceeded down Rodeo Drive. She didn't see any ear-piercing places either, but she had a pretty good feeling that if she brought the subject up, Camilla would be willing to take her somewhere to have it done. But she hesitated to broach the subject. Again, she didn't feel comfortable asking for things. Not yet.

Amy wondered if Nancy had come home from the university by now, if she'd found Amy's note. "What time is it?" she asked Camilla.

Camilla looked at her watch. "One-thirty. Why?"

"No reason," Amy said.

"Are you thinking about her?"

Amy was surprised. "My—Nancy?" How could Camilla have known? She thought about denying it, but Camilla was looking at her in such a kind, under-standing way.

"I just hope she's not too worried," Amy confessed.

"You should call her," Camilla said. "Let her know you're okay."

Amy was amazed at how thoughtful Camilla was. And obviously, she had no fear that Nancy would try to take Amy away. But why *should* Camilla be afraid of Nancy, if Camilla was Amy's real mother?

"You can use my mobile phone at lunch," Camilla told her. "And speaking of lunch, you must be starving!"

"No, I'm not," Amy protested. "I just ate a ton of egg salad sandwiches, remember?" But Camilla ignored her protests and led her up some stairs to a lovely terrace restaurant. Obviously Camilla was a regular. The man at the entrance greeted her warmly by name and immediately led her and Amy to a table.

Once they were seated, Camilla reached into her purse and drew out her mobile phone. "Here," she said, handing the phone to Amy. "I'm going to the ladies' room."

She was even making sure Amy had privacy! It gave Amy confidence as she dialed her own—what used to be her own—phone number. When she had finished dialing, she hesitated before hitting the button that would connect the call. This wasn't going to be an easy conversation. Nancy would be upset. But Amy hardened herself. Nancy had to have known the truth about Amy's parentage all along.

And there was one thing Amy knew for sure. Nancy wouldn't call the police and declare that Amy was a runaway.

In the past, even when Amy had been threatened and in real danger, Nancy had refused to call the police or any other authorities. She'd claimed they could be more dangerous than the organization. If legitimate agencies learned of Amy's existence, they could come up with legal reasons to take Amy away from Nancy.

But Amy had left Nancy of her own free will. And since she knew that a battalion of armed police officers weren't going to appear and drag her back, she had nothing to fear. She punched the connection button.

She was so ready to talk, it was almost disappointing to hear a busy signal. She wondered whether Nancy was calling all over town, going crazy, trying to find out if anyone knew where she was. Well, Amy would have been more than happy to tell her. It was Nancy's own fault for not having call waiting.

Camilla returned to the table. "Everything okay?" she asked.

Amy nodded, and Camilla didn't pursue the matter. She wasn't nosy at all. Nancy, on the other hand, questioned Amy about everything, wanting to know every tiny little detail of her life.

Camilla picked up the menu. "Now, what shall we have?"

Amy looked at her own menu. It was huge and over-whelming. Camilla must have read her expression.

"Would you like me to order for both of us?" she asked.

"Yes, please," Amy said.

"Let's see," Camilla mused. "No smoked salmon, of course."

As Camilla studied the menu, Amy studied her. She wondered how long it would take before she could look at Camilla's face and automatically think *Mother*. A powerful sensation of pure wonderment came over her. How very odd and thrilling it was to think that this was a blood relation sitting across from her.

As a child, of course, Amy had assumed that Nancy was her natural mother, but it had never occurred to her to look for physical similarities. And after Nancy had presented her version of Amy's creation, Amy had known there wouldn't be any similarities. But now she looked at Camilla and tried to see something of herself.

It wasn't in their coloring. Camilla had blond hair and blue eyes. Camilla's nose was longer than hers, and her cheekbones were higher. But maybe Amy would grow into those features.

Camilla looked up. "What are you looking at?"

"You," Amy said.

Camilla smiled. "I hope you like what you see."

"I do," Amy replied promptly. "But I was just thinking . . . I don't look much like you, do I?"

The smile on Camilla's face seemed to fade slightly. "Lots of children don't look like their parents."

"And I guess the medication you took might have had an effect on my appearance," Amy mused.

Camilla returned her gaze to the menu.

"About that medication," Amy went on. "I know it was experimental, but it seems to me that it would have become very popular if it could make your baby stronger and—"

"Do you like lamb?" Camilla interrupted. "The lamb chops here are delicious."

Amy agreed to lamb chops, and Camilla gave their order to the waiter. Then she turned her full attention back to Amy.

"Oh, Laura, there's so much I want to know about you. What you like to eat, what you like to do, your hobbies, your favorite flower, your favorite color . . . Do you like pink? I'm crazy about pink."

"Pink's okay," Amy said. She wouldn't have called it her favorite color, but she could deal with it.

"We've got a lot of bonding to do," Camilla went on. "It won't be easy, establishing the kind of relationship we should already have. Some people would probably suggest that we consult a psychologist for advice on getting along and becoming a family. But I don't like psychologists, do you?"

"I've never known any psychologists," Amy admitted.

"They think they know everything," Camilla told her. "Well, let me tell you, Laura, they're not as smart as they think they are."

Amy nodded uncertainly. She was still having trouble dealing with *Laura*.

The food came. Camilla was right about the lamb chops—they were delicious, and even though Amy wasn't famished she found herself wolfing them down happily. Camilla just picked at her salad, her bright eyes never leaving Amy's face.

"Tell me about your friends," Camilla said.

Now, that was a topic Amy could feel comfortable talking about. "My best friend, Tasha Morgan, lives right next door to me." She amended that. "Well, right next door to where I used to live."

"You'll miss her," Camilla said sympathetically.

Amy knew she would miss having easy access to her best friend, but she'd still be seeing her at school. That thought moved her to ask another question.

"How will I get to school every day?" she wondered aloud. "I can't walk to Parkside from here. Maybe there's a bus."

"Don't worry about that," Camilla told her. "Tell me more about your friends."

"Tasha's brother, Eric, is my boyfriend," Amy confided.

Something almost like a frown crossed Camilla's face. "Your boyfriend?"

"He's very nice," Amy assured her. "You'll like him."

"Boys," Camilla murmured. "They grow into men, you know."

Amy thought she was making a joke. "Yeah, I've heard about that."

But Camilla didn't smile. "You can't trust men, Amy. Believe me." She gave a short laugh. "I was married to one."

Amy visualized Dr. Jaleski. "Was he really that awful?" she asked. She still had a hard time accepting the idea of Dr. Jaleski as her father. And she had an even more difficult time picturing him as some sort of evil tyrant.

"He took you away from me," Camilla said simply. "I can never forget that." Her eyes filled up with tears, and the sight almost took Amy's breath away. This was her mother crying. This was the woman who had given birth to her, who had a natural love for her. A woman who had spent years in pain, searching for her beloved daughter. Everything went blurry, and Amy realized that she was crying too.

Camilla took some tissues from her purse and handed one to Amy. "Look at us, sobbing like babies," she said, laughing and crying at the same time.

"Thanks," Amy said, taking a tissue. "Thanks . . . Mom." It felt very weird, very foreign, using that word now, but she forced it out because she'd have to get used to it eventually. And it clearly made Camilla very, very happy. It produced a fresh onslaught of tears.

"We're going to be very happy, Laura," Camilla told her. She pushed the mobile phone across the table. "Would you like to call Tasha and Eric now?"

"Okay," Amy said, and she dialed the number. Tasha answered the phone.

"Hi," Amy said, "it's me."

"Amy!" Tasha gasped. "Where are you? Your mother's going crazy!"

"She's not my mother, Tasha," Amy said. "I'm *with* my mother."

"Ohhh, Amy," Tasha whispered. *"Where?"*

"In Beverly Hills, on Rodeo Drive," Amy began, but she stopped when she saw Camilla put a finger to her lips. She wasn't sure why she couldn't tell Tasha exactly where she was sitting at the moment. Camilla probably just didn't want any sort of confrontation.

"Don't tell Nancy, okay?" Amy said to Tasha. Camilla smiled at this and nodded in approval.

"I won't," Tasha said. "But she's really going nuts, Amy. She called here, and then she started asking me if I had any idea where you could be."

"What did you say?"

"I said I didn't know. I didn't tell her anything about Camilla."

Amy's heart filled with affection for her loyal best friend. "Thanks, Tasha."

"What's it like?" Tasha asked. "Finding your real mother . . ."

"It's . . . it's amazing," Amy said. "I don't know how else to describe it. I can't wait for you to meet her." As she said this, she smiled brightly at Camilla. But Camilla looked a little sad.

"This is so wonderful," Tasha moaned. "I hope Jeanine feels the same way you do. I think I found her natural mother."

"Really?"

"I found this adoption service on the Internet that matches people who are looking for their birth parents with parents looking for the children they put up for adoption. I put in all the details I have about Jeanine, and I got the name of a woman."

"Cool," Amy said, and as much as she disliked Jeanine, she hoped that her archenemy would know the happiness she herself was feeling right now.

Then, in the background on Tasha's end of the line, Amy heard the sound of a door slamming and a voice yelling.

"Hold on, Eric just got home and he's shouting about something," Tasha said to her, and then Amy heard her speaking to him. *"Calm down, she's okay!"* To Amy she said, "He just saw your mother, and—*Yes, it's Amy, wait a second, okay?"*

Amy wasn't surprised when Eric refused to wait. She could hear Tasha shriek as he wrestled the phone away from her.

"What's going on?" he demanded. "Where are you?" He sounded truly frantic.

"Everything's okay," Amy said soothingly. "More than okay. Stop yelling! Eric, I've found my mother. My real mother!"

She smiled at Camilla, but Camilla wasn't looking at her. She was asking the waiter for the check.

"Are you nuts?" Eric bellowed. "You're with that crazy lady right now?"

Amy stiffened. "She's not crazy, Eric."

"Amy, that woman's a wacko!"

"Don't talk about my mother like that!" Amy cried out. "She's not a wacko!"

"She's not your mother!" Eric yelled back, but his voice was more distant now. Camilla was taking the mobile phone out of Amy's hand, and she clicked the disconnect button.

"You see what I mean, Amy?" she said sadly. "Boys . . . men. They can't be trusted. Now he'll force his sister to tell him where you are, and he'll tell Nancy."

She was probably right. When Eric thought he knew

best, he could be awfully bossy. "I guess we'd better go," Amy said.

Camilla readily agreed. She paid the check, and then she took Amy's hand. Amy felt a little silly and childish, holding hands like that, but she didn't pull away. And she let Camilla lead her swiftly back to the bright blue sports car.

twelve 12

"Eric's not really that bad," Amy told Camilla as they sped down the freeway. "But he can get kind of macho sometimes. I think it's hard on him, having me as a girlfriend. Because I'm stronger than he is, you know? Once, when he sprained his ankle, I had to carry him on my back."

Camilla didn't respond. Her eyes were on the road, and Amy had to be grateful for that since they were going awfully fast. Amy sank back in the luxurious leather seat and said no more so Camilla could concentrate on driving. Neither of them spoke again until Camilla pulled into the underground parking lot of her high-rise building.

"Once Eric meets you, he'll feel a lot better about our being together," Amy said. "And when you get to know him, you'll like him too."

"I don't think that's going to happen, Laura," Camilla said.

"Sure it will," Amy insisted. "He's really not like most guys. He's a lot more sensitive."

Camilla laughed. "No, darling, what I'm saying is that I probably won't ever meet him." They were getting into the elevator, and Amy looked at her in dismay.

"What do you mean?"

"I think we should leave Los Angeles, Laura."

"Leave Los Angeles?" Amy was aware of sounding like a parrot, but she couldn't think of anything else to say.

They reached their floor, and Camilla unlocked the apartment door. "It's not safe for us here. Too many men who want to take you away from me. Eric. James . . ."

"Eric's not a man," Amy said. "And James . . . you mean Dr. J? He's *dead*!"

Camilla laughed. "I know that, darling. Don't mind me, I'm just thinking out loud." She took Amy's hand and pulled her to the sofa, where they sat side by side.

"We need to make a new life together, Laura, and we can't do it here. There are too many memories, too many people from our past. We have to make a fresh start. We need to go someplace where no one knows us, where they can accept us as mother and daughter."

Amy looked at her in bewilderment. "But—what about school?"

"There are schools everywhere, Laura."

She was right, of course. But Amy was still in a state of shock. She wanted to stay with Camilla, and she knew this would mean making a lot of changes in her life. But to move away from Los Angeles, from her school and her friends, and everything she knew . . .

"When do you want to move?" she asked.

"Now."

Amy caught her breath. "Now?"

Camilla smiled. "Not right this minute, darling. You didn't tell anyone where I live, did you?"

"No. I didn't know your address till you brought me here."

"And you didn't tell your friends just now on the phone," Camilla said. "What about Nancy?"

"I never talked to Nancy," Amy told her. "The line was busy. Maybe I should call her again."

"We need to pack," Camilla said. "Let's pack tonight and leave first thing in the morning, okay? You can call Nancy just before we leave, to say goodbye. Your friends too, of course."

Amy stared at her, unable to speak.

"We'll get a good night's sleep and take off bright and early," Camilla said.

"Where are we going?" Amy asked.

"I'm not sure," Camilla said pensively. Then she brightened. "We'll be vagabonds! You and me, we'll roam the world together. How does that sound?"

Amy was still speechless. Camilla took her hand.

"Darling, I know this all sounds shocking. But can't you see it's the best way for us? The only way? If we're going to have a future together, we have to get away from everything and everyone who's ever come between us. Do you understand that?"

Amy wasn't sure.

"I love to travel," Camilla said. "Have you ever been to the Grand Canyon?"

"No."

"It's breathtaking. The colors in the Southwest are like nothing you've ever seen before. The Petrified Forest, the Painted Desert—"

"What about school?"

"Travel is education," Camilla stated firmly. "You don't need a regular school like ordinary children. You're so special, you should be living like a special person. Oh, Laura, there's so much I could show you! Wouldn't you like to see Rome? London? Paris?"

"I know a little French," Amy ventured.

"Then we'll go to Paris first," Camilla declared. "You're going to love Paris! The grand boulevards, the cafés . . . We'll go to the top of the Eiffel Tower, and we'll take a boat ride down the Seine at night . . . would you like that?"

"Sure," Amy said, trying to take all this in.

"We'll roam the world, you and I. No one will ever separate us again. Never. We will be together forever."

Amy's head was spinning. She'd never heard talk like this before. But then, she'd never been loved like this before.

"Let's start packing," Camilla urged. "Right now!"

Amy nodded toward the little suitcase she'd dropped on the floor just hours earlier. "I'm already packed."

"Then you can help me pack," Camilla said. She took Amy to a bedroom, where she opened a closet and pulled out a suitcase. She began opening dresser drawers.

"Of course, I don't need everything, I can buy new clothes," she said. It sounded like she was talking more to herself than to Amy.

Doesn't she have a job? Amy wondered for the first time. Doesn't she have any ties that would keep her from leaving Los Angeles on a whim, just like that? What about this apartment? What about her friends?

Clearly, Camilla wasn't thinking about these things.

She pulled clothes out of the drawers and threw them on the bed. "Put these in the suitcase for me, Laura. No, wait, vagabonds don't need pantyhose. Oh, we're going to have so much fun! Let's not even wait for the morning. Let's leave tonight!"

Her mood was catching. And suddenly Amy began to feel like a vagabond too.

"Can we go to New Orleans?" she asked. "I saw a movie about New Orleans once."

"We'll be in New Orleans for Mardi Gras," Camilla said. "And we'll go to Brazil for Carnival! How about that?"

"It sounds like fun," Amy agreed. She could see herself buying postcards for Tasha and Eric, for Nancy, too, and mailing them from all over the world. And someday, once she and Camilla had bonded and felt like a real mother and daughter, they could come back, and Camilla could meet them all, and they could all be friends.

Amy stopped in the middle of folding a sweater. "Isn't that the doorbell?"

"No," Camilla said. She was in the closet now, picking out the shoes she wanted to pack.

But Amy heard the ringing again, loud and clear. "Someone's at the door, Camilla." She started out of the bedroom.

"No!" Camilla cried out, following her.

The ringing was persistent. "Who is it?" Amy called.

"Amy, it's me, it's your mother."

Camilla was just behind her. "She's not your mother!"

"I know," Amy said. "I know." She turned and faced Camilla earnestly. "But she tried to be my mother for twelve years. I have to see her. Don't worry, she won't make a terrible fuss, she's not like that."

Camilla sighed and nodded. Amy went to the door and opened it. Nancy stood there, pale but calm.

Amy stepped aside so she could come in. She was surprised to see that Nancy was not alone. Mary Jaleski came in behind her.

Amy heard Camilla make a choking sound.

"Hello, Camilla," Mary said in a pleasant voice. "It's been a long time." From her tone, they could have been bumping into each other in a supermarket aisle.

Amy stepped back to stand alongside Camilla. Her eyes darted back and forth between Nancy and Mary.

"I'm not going back with you," she told Nancy.

"I can't force you to come back," Nancy said. "But I want you to hear what Mary has to say."

"*You,*" Camilla said to Mary, and it was as if she spit out the word. "You are your father's daughter. Do you think you're going to take my baby away from me again in his name?"

Mary spoke gently. "My father didn't take anyone away from you, Camilla."

"Oh no?" Camilla challenged her. "Then why have I had to spend twelve years searching for my daughter?"

"Your daughter doesn't exist," Mary said. "Your daughter's dead."

"Come here, Laura," Camilla demanded, and Amy drew closer to her. She felt Camilla's arm around her shoulders, holding her tightly. "Look at her," Camilla said to Mary. "She's alive. Your father, the other doctor, that stupid psychologist, all of them, they tried to make me think she died, but I never believed them, never."

Amy looked at her in puzzlement. "What is Mary talking about?"

"It's nothing, don't listen to her, Laura," Camilla urged.

"That's not Laura, Camilla," Mary said. "Laura died three days after she was born."

Camilla hugged Amy more tightly. "That's what they told me. But it wasn't true. How could she die? She was perfect."

Mary spoke sadly. "You know why Laura died, Camilla."

Amy was watching Camilla's eyes. They were blank.

Nancy spoke. "Camilla was a drug addict, Amy. Dr. Jaleski tried to get her to stop taking drugs while she was pregnant, but she couldn't. When her daughter was born . . ." Her voice trailed off as if it was too painful to go on.

"Her child was severely damaged," Mary told Amy. "She couldn't survive."

"That's not true!" Camilla shrieked. "She was perfect! Your father was evil. He wanted me to think she died so he could do his experiments on her!"

Amy was completely bewildered. "That's not what you told me," she said to Camilla. "You said he divorced you and took custody of me."

Mary looked at Camilla with sympathy and compassion. "You had to tell yourself that, didn't you? Because you felt so guilty. You thought the drugs had destroyed your baby."

"Not true, not true, not true," Camilla chanted. "The drugs, they made her perfect, that's why he wanted to keep her, that's why he took her away."

Nancy turned to Amy. "Dr. Jaleski felt awful about what happened. He always thought he could have stopped Camilla from taking drugs if he'd been home more and not working at the laboratory so much. And the guilt was too much for Camilla. She had a complete breakdown, and she was committed to a psychiatric hospital. You've been in and out of hospitals ever since, haven't you, Camilla?"

Camilla laughed. "Psychiatrists, psychologists, they're

all idiots, they don't know a thing. They kept telling me to accept that my daughter was dead. But I wouldn't. And I was right, because here she is!" She pulled Amy around so they were facing each other. "Don't listen to them, Laura. Your father was an evil man! He's the one who was crazy, not me!"

Mary continued to speak in a low voice. "You knew my father, Amy. You know he wasn't evil. In fact, even after they were divorced, he continued to support Camilla. In his will, he left her enough money so she could always be cared for."

Nancy drew closer. "That's how I found out where you were, Amy. Mary called me. She was concerned when you asked her about Camilla. And she had Camilla's address, because the checks from her father's estate go to Camilla every month." She was speaking softly too, as if she was trying to keep Camilla from hearing what she said.

Amy looked up into Camilla's face and realized that their efforts weren't necessary. Camilla wasn't hearing anything they said. There was a glaze over her eyes.

"Camilla?" Amy whispered. "Mom?"

Suddenly Camilla's arms tightened even closer around Amy. For such a small, delicate woman, she was surprisingly strong. "Get out of here," she said through her teeth. "Get out of here and leave us alone!" She started to move backward, pulling Amy with her.

Amy could see Mary's face change. Now she was more alarmed than compassionate. "You can't get away, Camilla. We won't let you out the door."

"We'll go out on the terrace," Camilla said. "Yes, that's what we'll do! We'll leave from the terrace. Then we can be together forever and ever, Laura. Forever and ever!"

She was extremely strong. Her fingers felt like steel rods. Amy had once read that mentally unbalanced people could exert unusual strength. She had to use real force, serious energy, to break away from Camilla. And with every ounce of resistance, she could feel her heart breaking.

Camilla didn't try to stop her. She didn't even move. With her arms extended, she moaned, "Laura, Laura. My baby. I killed my baby."

Mary went closer to her and put an arm around her. "You don't know that's true, Camilla. It might have been the drugs that injured Laura, but it could have been something else, something you couldn't do anything about."

Did Camilla even hear her? Did she understand what Mary was saying? Amy couldn't be sure. All she could see in Camilla's eyes was madness. And Camilla went completely limp as Mary led her out of the apartment.

"Camilla?" Amy whispered as she passed. And then . . . "Mother?"

But Camilla moved right past her, as if she didn't even see her anymore.

Amy looked at Nancy. She could see compassion in her eyes, but now it was directed at her.

"You'll come home with me?" Nancy posed it as a question, not a statement. She was giving Amy a choice.

Amy knew she didn't have any option. But she also knew that she didn't need one.

thirteen

Amy woke up unusually early the next day. Normally on a Sunday morning she liked to lie in bed and think, but there was nothing she wanted to think about that morning. Memories of the day before were too fresh and painful.

On the way home, there had been no more talk of being grounded. Nancy didn't seem to expect any explanation or apology from Amy. She treated Amy gently, almost as if she was a fragile bird. Which she was, in a way. She needed recovery time. Very little had been said. And when they'd arrived home, all Amy had wanted to do was go to bed, where she fell right away into a sound and dreamless sleep.

Now, wide awake, she went quietly out of her room so she wouldn't wake Nancy when she passed her door, and she tiptoed down the stairs.

But Nancy was already there, sitting at the kitchen table. When she saw Amy, she smiled. "Good morning."

"Good morning," Amy replied.

"Would you like some juice?"

"Yes, thank you."

How strangely they were speaking to each other, like polite acquaintances. In silence, Nancy sipped her tea and Amy drank her orange juice. Amy tried to remember how they used to talk at breakfast. It all seemed very long ago and far away. This person sitting across from her at the table, with lines of concern etched into her forehead . . . Amy wasn't sure who she was anymore. She wasn't even sure who she herself was.

But the silence was too hard to take. Amy broke it. "How did she know about me?" There was no need to explain who she meant by *she*.

"Mary found a letter in Camilla's handbag," Nancy said. "An anonymous letter, with information about you. Your phone number, address, school. We think it might have come from the organization."

"Why would the organization write to Camilla?"

"They may have felt she would be more vulnerable to being persuaded to work with them. More willing to let them know you. At least, more willing than I would ever be."

"Oh." It made sense, Amy supposed. And with Camilla wanting so desperately to change the past, to think her child had never died, she would definitely be ready to believe whatever might confirm this. "She's not a bad person, you know. I know now that she was sick. But not bad."

Nancy nodded. "And she loved you very much."

But Amy knew better. "She loved the person she thought I was."

Nancy didn't argue with her.

"Have you ever seen a movie called *Laura*?" Amy asked suddenly.

"Yes. It's about a woman who everyone thinks is dead. But she turns out to be alive. It's very romantic."

"Not very realistic?"

"No, not very realistic."

When she had finished her juice, Amy went back upstairs to shower and dress. Then she selected a favorite old book from her shelf, *Charlotte's Web*, and curled up on her bed to read the familiar story of Wilbur, the little pig who needed a mother—or at least, someone who acted like a mother. Wilbur found that mother figure in a spider named Charlotte. Not very realistic. And yet totally believable.

Amy tried to read slowly, like a regular person, but she'd read the book so many times that she practically knew it by heart. And she knew what was coming, so she started to cry even before the story became truly sad. She was so engrossed, she didn't even hear the bell downstairs.

A moment later Nancy rapped at her door. "Amy? Tasha and Eric are here. Do you want to see them?"

So she wasn't forbidden company anymore. "All right," she said.

Her best friend and her boyfriend entered her room silently. Both looked awkward, embarrassed, and very happy to see her.

"You okay?" Eric asked gruffly.

"I'm fine." It was a lie, and Amy knew that Eric knew it was a lie, but for now it would have to do. Tasha, however, was more willing to express herself. She burst into tears and threw her arms around her best friend.

"I was such an idiot!" she cried. "I feel like it's all my fault!"

"How could it be your fault?" Amy asked her.

"I showed you that birth certificate!"

Amy shrugged. "That didn't change anything. I believed what I wanted to believe."

"But I wish I had kept researching," Tasha said. "I might have found this, too." She handed Amy a paper, another computer printout. Only this one was a certificate of death. For Laura Jean Jaleski, three days old.

Amy read it carefully, then put it aside. "I hope Jeanine's search turns out better," she said, but Tasha was already shaking her head.

"I gave Jeanine the information I found, but she didn't care. She doesn't even want to call the woman! She said she's not interested in being the daughter of someone ordinary. She told me to keep looking until I came up with royalty or a movie star."

"Well, at least you'll make more money," Amy said.

Tasha shook her head. "I told her I couldn't guarantee anything. So she said maybe she was better off with the parents she had. At least they love her. And they're rich."

Despite the way she was feeling, Amy couldn't help herself—she burst out laughing. That was just *so* Jeanine.

"Then she refused to pay me for the work I'd done," Tasha told her.

Amy could believe that. It was also typical Jeanine.

"So it looks like I won't be getting my ears pierced anytime soon," Tasha said mournfully. "Well, that's okay. I'd rather wait until we can do it together. Maybe you should ask your mother again—"

Eric looked at her fiercely. "Tasha!"

Tasha stopped and flushed. "I'm sorry."

"Sorry for what?" Amy asked. Then she knew. "You can say *mother* in front of me. It's okay."

They didn't stay much longer. They had to visit their grandparents, and Amy was glad to get back to *Charlotte's Web*. But after a few minutes she put the book aside and went downstairs.

Nancy was in the living room, reading the newspaper. She looked up and smiled when Amy came in.

"You're not working on your proposal?" Amy asked.

Nancy shook her head. "No, I'm finished with all that. Either they promote me or they don't. I'm not going to think about it anymore. It's not the most important thing in my life."

"It's not?"

"No! Amy, do you know what is the most important thing in any mother's life? Her child." And in Nancy's eyes, Amy saw all the love she had thought she saw in Camilla's. Only Camilla loved Laura, a fantasy. Nancy loved the real thing.

Never in a million years had Amy thought she would ever learn something from Jeanine. But on this day, Amy owed Jeanine her thanks. Because Amy too now realized she was far better off with the parent she had.

fourteen

That night Amy had a dream, a vivid and familiar dream. The glass incubator, the bright flames of fire around her, the heat, the intense fear . . . and then the arms carrying her away. The face looking down at her with all the love in the world, the kind of love only a mother can have for a child.

Mother. Not through blood. But through love.

Don't miss

replica

#9
The Fever

Amy has never been sick a day in her life. Superior genes guarantee her perfect health. But suddenly she's experiencing pain, dizziness, and loss of physical control. It's totally baffling—and alarming. And since Amy can't risk seeing a doctor, it's up to her mother to find the cause of Amy's condition.

With her fever rising every second, Amy's head whirls with questions:

Why are her amazing skills disappearing just when she needs them most?

What if she survives only to live as an ordinary teenager?

What if her mother can't find a cure—because someone doesn't want her to?

What if there *is* no cure?

The answers aren't pretty. All Amy knows is that she'll fight till the end.